I Want Doesn't Get

I Want Doesn't Get

RONY ROBINSON

faber and faber

LONDON · BOSTON

For Goronwy

First published in 1991
by Faber and Faber Limited
3 Queen Square London WC1N 3AU

Photoset by Parker Typesetting Service, Leicester
Printed in Great Britain by Clays Ltd, St Ives plc

A CIP record for this book is available from the
British Library

ISBN 0 571 16245 2

Part One

1 When My Amazing Mother Vanished

I was having sausages for tea with my father and sisters, on the second Friday in September.

Eliza said, 'Sausages are cruel. Nicky says.'

I said, 'Nicky's in London.'

'Not.'

'Is.'

'Was,' said my father. 'Isn't now.'

'Where is she now then?' I asked.

'She's . . . gone round the world.'

And that's what happened when my amazing mother vanished.

There used to be six of us at Number 77.

1 My father, who worked at a building society and wore shiny suits and aftershaves. A young woman once queued for money at his window, and then became –

2 my mother, Nicky.

And not long after, she came with him to Number 77 to have –

3 – me, Julian, and my –

4   – five-year-old sister Eliza, who went to
     playgroup, and her –
5   – two-year-old sister Madge, who stayed at
     home with Nicky.
And then there was –
6   – Chonk the cat, who killed things in the
     garden.

That garden had a bald lawn, a broken swing, a
leaning fence, and the animal graveyard right at
the top under the bluebells under the trees. I'd not
dared go there since I was six.

Nicky blamed me for the bald lawn, and my
father for everything else, including the bubbly
tarmac at the front where she parked her canary
yellow Citroën CV car, with the flappy windows.

Mrs Embleton lived at Number 79, and grumbled
about her rhubarb. The Rogersons lived behind the
hedge at Number 75, played the piano, said good
morning,[1] and didn't notice when my mother
vanished, and we all went peculiar.[2]

[1] *If it was morning.*
[2] *But just before we did go peculiar (once this story really
    begins):*
    ● *I'd just gone up into Mr Hills's class. He said my
    handwriting was like a baboon's but he liked my
    vocabulary work with the dictionary and reference
    books.*

4

Anyway, at twenty to twelve on that Friday night when she vanished, I found my father blowing smoke into the cooker.

'*Has* Nicky really gone round the world?' I asked.

'Yes.'

'How?'

There were black smudges round his pink eyes. 'She was in London. She saw an offer of cheap round-the-world plane tickets. She sold the canary car . . . She went.'

'How do you know?'

'She rang from the airport.'

'When?'

'Very early yesterday morning.'

'How long's she going for?'

'She didn't say.'

'What are we supposed to do without her?'

'She didn't say that either. It might help if you can open a window, we're on fire.'

'Shouldn't open windows when there's a fire.'

_____

- *I'd just fallen out with Jamie Learmouth because of the shirt.*
- *I was happy but I didn't know I was (till I wasn't).*
- *All I* wanted *was: a dog; another chance to play in the cubs' football team; a brother. But, 'I* want *doesn't get', like mums say, even mine . . .*

5

2 Going Peculiar

My two-year-old sister Madge went peculiar in a
peculiar way, but only at nights.

I'd read her her sleepy story. She'd shut her eyes.
I'd say sleep-tight-mind-the-bed-bugs. I'd tiptoe
out. She'd stand up. I'd run back to stop her. She'd
crack her head against the wall. I'd read her a sleepy
story. She'd shut her eyes. I'd say etc.

Some nights there was one big brain-crack every
twenty minutes. Some nights she went at it like a
woodpecker.[1]

Whenever I woke in the night (which was often)
she'd be cracking away. When I moved her cot away
from the wall, she cracked herself on the cot corners
instead.

[1] *Woodpeckers: There are three kinds of Woodpecker in
Britain but none in Ireland. They peck to make nests.
They're called 'yaffles' sometimes, because of their
horrible laugh. The greater spotted woodpecker used to be
extinct but it isn't any more. (I don't understand how.)*

6

It happened every night for months.

My father stayed off work, going peculiar. He
padded round in his dressing gown and bare feet
worrying the cooker. He stopped wearing his
glasses after he stamped on them. He bumped
things instead. And changed.

Eliza went peculiar quietest, trailing round with all
her lions, tigers, dogs, cats, pandas, horses,
alligators, monkeys, dolls, lambs, llamas, teddies,
rabbits and bears. She'd line them behind curtains
and under tables, add them up, and comfort them.
Next day, she'd scatter them all over the house,
and start again.

Chonk went peculiar by sleeping in Nicky's shoes
at the bottom of her wardrobe and biting up at her
dangling clothes.

I still went to school, so nobody noticed how
peculiar I was getting.
    But on the second Thursday dinner time after
Nicky vanished, Mr Hills was on playground duty.
I didn't see him till he was right in front of me with
a saucer on his teacup.
    'Um – a windy one, Julian?'
    'Yes.'
    'About a number 5 on the Beaufort Wind Scale,

7

would you say?' He explained the Beaufort Wind Scale.[2]

'Oh,' I said.

'So um how *are* things at home, Julian?'

'All right.'

'Your mum?'

'Gone round the world.'

'Your shirt looked um a bit wet round the collar this morning?'

'My father can't make the spin dryer spin.'

'And you're always late?'

'My father can't drive.' I looked into the wind Mr Hills was so interested in. 'He's useless. But he'll have to go back to his building society soon. Then we can be taken into care like the Squireses keep being.'

He sipped his tea in the wind. 'Haven't you any um relations who can help?'

'My mum's mum and dad are in Glasgow.'

'Scotland um?' Mr Hills nodded and explained the differences between Glasgow and Edinburgh.

'Oh.'

'Um . . . so how long do you think your mother is going to be away, Julian?'

'As long as it takes to get round the world, s'pose.'

[2] *If it's 0 there's no wind. If it's 12 there's no you.*

8

'Eighty days? Like in the story?'[3]

He explained the story. I added eighty days from the Thursday she'd got the plane, and worked out that she would be back in the early morning of 11 December.[4]

Then he gave me his empty cup and saucer, and said I could take it back to the staff room for him.

He touched my elbow as I turned. 'The other children being um all right, Julian?'

'Course.'

'I wondered why you were playing on your own?'

'Cos I want to,' I lied. 'This wind's making my eyes run, Mr Hills. It must be Beaufort Scale 6 now, easy.'

'You hold on to my cup then.'

I did, most of the way.

[3] *By Jules Verne.*
[4] *If October had thirty-one days.*

3   Elephant Knickers

I was eating gunge[1] in front of the telly at half
past nine that night when my father came in with
Nicky's ironing board and tried to put it up.

I asked if he fancied a game of snooker.

I'd only asked to be kind. He was useless at
snooker too. Proper fathers have to cheat to let
their own kids win. It was the other way round in
our house.

He went peculiar.

'How can I possibly play snooker?' he yelled.
'With all this ironing? You do know the cooker's
gone out again? Who's doing all the shopping?
What about the spin dryer door? It won't open
now, and all my clothes are still inside. How can I

[1] *Without Nicky, we ate gunge all the time, e.g. one
Sunday all we had was: soft fig biscuits; smoked
barbecue crisps; frozen black forest gateau; an old salami
and a tin of plums in an opened rusty tin; a milk shake of
tinned milk, strawberry jam and white sugar cubes I'd
once made dice out of, with felt tip; lots more.*

read the instructions without my glasses? How can I get my glasses mended if I've no clothes? And – '

The phone rang in the kitchen.

'And the phone's ringing in the kitchen,' I said.

He swore.

And that *was* peculiar.[2]

I slurped gunge and waited for him to come back and say Nicky was on the phone.

She wasn't.

'It was your Mr Hills from school. About your shirt.' He scorched his thumb on the iron. 'You've been stupid, Julian.'

I shrugged.

He said, 'If I can't manage, you do know what'll happen?'

I shrugged. 'You're burning Eliza's elephant knickers.'

'There are more important things than burnt knickers.' But he banged the scorched elephants.

'Tell Eliza that.'

'Do you *want* to be split up?'

'Nobody asks me what I want.'

'If that's what you do want – '

'I want doesn't get.'

[2] *Nicky was the swearer in our family, specially about e.g. gunge eating, the government, doorbells, Christmas, aftershaves, dogs, beards, men, and boys. She was a brilliant swearer actually.*

11

' – all you have to do is let everyone know what a hard time you're having and how useless I am. Do you understand?'

I peered round him at the telly.

'Look at me,' he yelled.

I looked. He was very pale.

'Do you *understand*?'

'Yes!' I lied.

I was spending Saturday afternoon booting my torn football, when Mrs Embleton popped up in her rhubarb.

'Is that you, young Julian?'

'Think so, Mrs Embleton.'

'What mischief you up to?'

'Kicking.'[3]

When I was little, and she was bigger, and everything was all right, her husband used to smoke his pipe at the end of these gardens. And she used to give me barley sugars.

'What's your mother up to, young Julian, that's what I want to know?'

'How'd you mean, Mrs Embleton?'

'She was for ever *banging* about, your mother. Why's she stopped, eh?'

[3] *Even I couldn't turn a ball 360 degrees into her rhubarb, even if I was brilliant, even if I had been unfairly dropped by the cubs. (I had.)*

12

'She's got a job, Mrs Embleton. I think it's in . . .
Doncaster.'

'Where's her funny yellow car gone then?'

'She had to sell it because she's in a . . . glove
factory you see? Working nights.'

'I used to work nights on them cranes in the
steelworks in the war you know.'

I did know. I said, 'Did you, Mrs Embleton?'

She told me, sounding like she used to when
there were still barley sugars and pipe smoke at the
bottom of our gardens and –

'And you tell your mother to eat right, and she'll
not go far wrong, working nights.'

'I'll tell her.'

'And you tell her I was getting worried with her
not banging about. Because, say what you like
about your mother, she's not a quiet woman.'

'No need to worry,' I lied, like my father said I
had to.

Three Saturday mornings after, I was breakfasting
on sultanas and lime juice, and watching some daft
kids on telly stamping balloons and shrieking.

Eliza came in wearing Nicky's high heels. And
nothing else. She squodged up on the brown sofa
with the broken springs, and said I was her best
brother.[4] But then she got silly.

[4] *I was, then.*

13

I told her, quietly. She just said, 'No *you* silly.'
She climbed onto the sofa back.
So I said, quietly, she musn't.
'No, *you* billy!'
So I said quietly that if she fell she'd end up in the children's hospital and the doctors'd ask where her mother was, and then we'd all be taken into care.
'You Pilly!' she said.
And then, 'Filly!'
She stood on the sofa back, in Nicky's high heels.
So I said, quietly, that if she was going to be silly we would all end up in different orphanages.
'Nilly! Jilly! Hilly!'
I said quietly that when we were old we'd walk past each other in the road and –
'Willy!' She dived, ripped one high heel in the sofa, and stabbed the other in my elbow. I grabbed as she flew past, and just stopped her cracking her brains on the coffee table.
She lay yelling she was blind, till my father came down with Madge yelling on his head.
'For heaven's sake what is going on in here? I can't be everywhere at once. What's this rip in the sofa? What's this mess on the floor? What's *wrong* with you, Julian?'
I yelled that there was nothing wrong with me, actually. I had just stopped Eliza committing

14

suicide actually. She yelled that I'd blinded her. Madge slithered into my lime juice, and yelled about that.

I yelled it wasn't fair, I was only trying to watch my programme actually.

My father yelled, 'I'll tell you what's not fair, *actually*, and it's you who's not fair laddie. You can't even sit watching television while I do all the work, can you? I thought I'd explained it to you very clearly? Is this what you want?'

'I want doesn't g–'

And he hit me. Smack on my cheek, punch on my shoulder. Kick on my ankle.

He'd never ever hit us before.

We all stopped yelling, even the daft kids stamping balloons.

Eliza was the first to speak. 'When's Nicky coming home? . . . Want Nicky . . . And who burned my elephants?'

4 She Frowned At Me

I kept *hearing* Nicky.

E.g. I was in my room beating myself at snooker. There was a bang at the front door. I called, 'Nicky? I'm going for the pink, so don't you rush in and –'

I stayed folded over the table, till she smacked open the door, and dived me onto my bed.

'Get off me!'

But she wouldn't. She shouted, 'Hate kissing, don't you? Afraid of your feelings? But we all need cuddles, we all need squodging!'

And she cuddled and squodged, and I suffocated in her Apricot Kernel smell-without-cruelty stuff all night.

Only – she wasn't really there.

Or e.g. I was watching telly. Feet stomped down the hall. There was some swearing. I grabbed for the Thing, and cried, 'I'm not watching telly Nicky. I know it's only mindless macho rubbish,

16

and I would like to learn the piano like you said
Nicky only please don't squodge me – '[1]

I stood blind and shipwrecked between the telly
and the brown sofa with the broken springs.

But she did not come.

So in the end I opened my eyes, sat and watched
some more mindless macho telly rubbish. Or just
sat.

Or e.g. I was sitting at her make-up mirror,
dabbing her Apricot Kernel on my wrists, and
wearing her clothes. Too late I saw her reflection.

'Mercy Nicky! I'm only little really and – '

'Think you can sneak in here and pinch my
things, do you? Thief! *Man*! I'm going to . . . do
you!'

But she never did.

And then, one really rotten night full of a really
rotten dream that kept going round and round, I
woke up terrified.

Time had stopped. It was going to be dark for
ever.

I had wet the bed again of course. But it wasn't
that.

[1] *I've seen her wrestle a building society clerk onto the
floor and jump on him, singing liberation songs till he
needed the doctor.*

Madge was head-cracking every seventeen seconds. It wasn't that either.

I dared not move.

I had forgotten what she looked like.

What colour had her hair been the night before she went to London? Orange? No, because she'd been more careful with the henna after the trouble last summer when she'd held my father over the bath and turned him tangerine by mist–

And what colour were her *eyes*?

I pressed my own, very tight, to see her again. And couldn't.

I tiptoed to the little room where Nicky kept her sewing machine, bottle collection, old letters, files, free offers, posters, buttons, plants, newspaper parcels, viola, pressed flowers, yoghurt maker, badge board and, somewhere, her old photographs.

I found a stuck down envelope of 'Us!', but that was only their love letters, from before me. His were one side of paper, in his best handwriting. Hers were pages long, in different coloured inks, with drawings and kisses. Some of the letters had been torn, and stuck together again.

I found the old photographs in a file marked 'Old Photographs'.

The best was a tiny one of her in a check school uniform. She was probably only four or five years

18

older than me, frowning, and freckly. Her skin wasn't quite a real pink. Her hair was bubbly, and nearly ginger. And her eyes were . . . greeny blueyish.

I stared at her.

She frowned back, from before I was born, as if she could tell what was coming, including me.

I rummaged on through her papers. What I really wanted[2] now was the secret letter to me marked SECRET AND PRIVATE, with the secret details of how to meet her at some secret place at some secret time, soon, and how I'd secretly recognize her there and stay secretly with her for ever.

I found no more secrets.

So I stuck her, frowning and freckly, at the back of the second shelf of the red and white striped cupboard she had painted for me.

I piled Beanos in front of her, and went to have a bath, and hide my wet pajamas.

[2] *(and didn't get, of course).*

5 Like My Toes?

And then Eliza started actually talking to her.

It was the Monday morning of half term. My father was trying to mend the lavatory seat that somebody[1] had deliberately tilted off by sitting down too hard. He'd found Nicky's toolbox, then a key to it, then her Encyclopaedia of Do-It-Yourself, and now, days later he was Doing-It.

Madge was asleep. She always was in the day, so she could be awake for the head-cracking at night.

My plan had been to ring up some kids from school, but Eliza was already in the kitchen, squatting under the blackboard, talking into the phone.

'. . . and lots and lots of fireworks! But I'll not hold them, only the easy ones and I will be very careful Nicky and – '

Nicky?

Eliza stuck her thumb up her pink leotard, and

[1] *Me.*

20

looked under her bottom to see where she had left her feet. She waved, like Nicky used to when she sat there in *her* leotard all morning doing yoga and telephoning people.

Eliza nodded at the phone, '. . . yes, and Julian is a very good boy only he does wee the bed now and Madge is trying to stop hitting but Chonk can't go to the doctor with her fleas because Daddy has broken his glasses.'

I bit my nails.[2]

'. . . Yes,' she said.

And then, '. . . Oh yes!'

And then, 'I can go and be a ballet dancer when I grow up can't I, Nicky? I'll eat lots of hotyog. Night night.'

I leaned towards her. 'It's not night, it's quarter to eleven in the morning[3] and – '

Eliza kissed the phone and ballet-danced to the fridge.

I lifted the phone. There was only the brrrrrrr, now.

Eliza said, 'Please may you open this hotyog for me, Julian?'

I lifted her onto the kitchen table, got two dirty

[2] *What was left of them.*
[3] *It was quarter to eleven at night* somewhere *of course, e.g. Australia. Was she there, half way round the world, already?*

spoons from the sink and we began the very last yoghurt ever.[4]

'You can have it all,' I said. 'Did you ring Nicky?'

Eliza splashed. 'This hotyog tastes of sick.'

'It doesn't.'

'You eat it!'

'All right,' I said, pretending. 'If Nicky comes on the phone again, can I have a talk with her as well?'

'Say please?'

'Please.'

'You're not eating your hotyog?'

I licked the spoon, and knocked the rest onto the floor.

On the Wednesday morning I put on my United kit to go training in the garden, ready for when I got the recall to the cub squad. I was also ready with the news for Mrs Embleton that my mother had lost her job at the Doncaster glove factory for striking against humans abusing dead animals, and was now working in –

But I didn't even get outside.

Eliza was sitting naked on the kitchen table, on the phone again.

'Mr Monkey's been naughty, Nicky. I've told him he must eat if he wants to grow up to be a big

[4] *It tasted of banana and sick.*

22

strong girl. I must go now Nicky because there is someone at the door.'

'No!' I cried, too late.

She kissed the phone and smacked it down again.

'Not fair!' I yelled. 'You promised I could speak to her if she was on the phone again.'

'Can.' She passed it.

Brrrr.

'Was it Nicky?' I said.

'Yes.'

'How did you know it was *her*?'

'Cos she's my mummy.'

And on Sunday afternoon –

'Who is it on the phone?'

'Nobody.'

'Who *was* it then?'

'Nicky. Look, can lick my toes.'

'She wasn't really here, was she?'

'Who?'

'Nicky?'

'Course not,' she said. But then she added, 'She was in the phone.'

The following Tuesday my teeth started crumbling because of the fluoride pills Nicky used to force us to take before she forced us not to take them after she went to a meeting. My mouth gunged with

23

chocolate, fluoride, and blood. And Debbie Henderson from our class said she'd never kiss me with a mouthful of blood and chocolate and –

And I woke up on the floor, desperate for a fizzy drink. I went down to find Eliza snaked in the phone cable. She smelt of wet[5] pajamas.[6]

'Julian here now.'

I said, 'I've come for a fizzy drink because of the chocolate and blood.'

'He says chocolate and blood, Nicky.'

I fizzed her an apple, and held it out. 'You'll need both hands.'

We swapped phone for fizzy.

I said, 'Nicky?'

Brrrrrrr.

'Nicky – can you hear me. I'm Julian.'

Brrrrr.

I said, 'She's not there.'

Eliza gulped fizzy up her nose. Then down. I wiped her and we swapped back.

Eliza said, 'Hello Nicky. Julian can't do the phone.'

[5] *Just like me.*
[6] *The English spelling is 'pyjamas'. I've had an argument with Mr Hills about it. But the word comes from Urdu and Persian, because they invented pajamas, and called them 'pajamas'. So so do I.*

I said, 'Ask her what time it is where she is because . . .'[7]

'What time is it, Nicky? . . . She can't see.'

'Is it dark where she is?'

'I can't see.'

'Where is she?'

'Ask her.'

'She can't see.'

'Is it a long way away?'

'Yes.'

'When will she be home?'

'You ask.'

We swapped.

I said, 'Nicky you know December 11th, well if you take eighty days from when you set off to go round the – ?'

Brrrrrr.

I shook my head at Eliza. 'Nicky not there.'

'She's gone back to bed.'

'Oh.' I kissed the phone. 'Night night then Nicky. Sleep tight and mind the bed bugs don't. Amen.'

We swapped.

Eliza said, 'Night night Nicky . . . Not Nicky now.'

'Who is it?'

[7] '. . . *if we know what time it is where she is we can work out where she is.*'

25

'. Postman Pat now!'[8]

We swapped.

Brrrr.

I said, 'Oh I am so sorry to hear that Pat. But why would Ted Glenn want to cut off Jess's tail? Oh I see, because he doesn't believe it's fair to have pets because pets aren't ecological.'[9]

Eliza said, '*Is* it Postman Pat?'

'Course.'

'Really?'

'Really as Nicky.'

'Has he a letter for me?'

'He says no but there will soon be a letter for both of us, with foreign stamps.'

We stayed up for ages.[10]

At twenty past five, I got some dry pajamas for both of us and we went back to bed.

We often played talking-to-Nicky after that, when we were on our own.

[8] *i.e. it's not true.*

[9] *Nicky's opinion too. Both wrong.*

[10] *We talked to e.g. a) United's goalkeeper who said he was sorry for the season so far, and I told him how to anticipate the ball; b) Mrs Embleton, and I told her about the glove factory, and how Nicky had now got a job selling chocolate teeth in Bridlington; c) Jamie Learmouth and frightened him.*

Part Two

6   Not Much Of A Day

Dinner time on the fourth Saturday without Nicky.

Outside the library, with bits of frozen shopping in heavy carrier bags drooping off the handles of the double buggy. My father with frozen shopping and milk bottles poking out of his coat pocket. Rain.

There were four kids peeping through the steamy window:

1 and 2   Two Squires kids who didn't matter,
3   Natalie Thingy who did,
4   . . . Debbie Henderson!

My father banged the double buggy forwards into the glass door, stubbed Eliza's toes, turned it backwards and trapped Madge's fingers.

Natalie Thingy yaffled like a woodpecker.

My father banged sideways into Adults's, leaving mud right up to the counter where Mrs Beacon stood daring anyone to breathe on her books.

Natalie was now skulking behind by an empty bookcase called New Fiction. And whispering, loud, 'There's that Julian Chandler from our class whose mother's run off! And his Dad's banging into things! And just look at the state of them all!'

My father unloaded books at Mrs Beacon's counter.

Eliza untied herself and ran into Children's. The buggy fell backwards with the weight of the frozen shopping, but without the weight of Eliza. Madge fell, screamed, and went back to sleep in one breath.

Natalie yaffled, behind Romance.

Mrs Beacon said, 'There are *thirty-one* books here Mr Chandler. Thirty-one books are not permitted.'

'*Mrs* Chandler took them out.'

Mrs Beacon opened the books. 'These were due back in April.'

'Yes.'

'They are wet.'

'It's raining outside.'

His neck between hat and collar was very red. I strolled into the middle of the library so that no one would think I was with him.

'He's blushing like his dad,' Natalie whispered, stepping out from behind LARGE PRINT. 'But we've got to be nice to him, haven't we? Hello Julian Chandler.'

'Dooly Shandy!'[1] called a Squires.

[1] *Julian Chandler*.

I strolled back to my father, so that no one would think I was with them.

Mrs Beacon was talking more loudly than she allows *us* to. 'I'm afraid I cannot go round the world after her, Mr Chandler.'

'Quite,' my father said.

'And I am also afraid that if we are not careful your whole family will be invalidated.'

'I'm afraid of that too.'

I stroked Madge's wet hair.

Natalie and Co. went, 'Aaaaaah.'

Mrs Beacon said, 'Twelve pounds thirty pence, including the postage for the three reminders.'

'Right then here we – oops.' My father almost tipped the milk bottle, as he lifted his coat to dig for money from his back pocket. A bag of frozen peas splonked onto Madge. She was getting used to him, and didn't even bother to wake up to grumble.

I strolled into Children's, hoping to see Miss Day the Children's librarian. But I couldn't see her, only her purple cardigan,[2] under the Infants Easy

[2] *Nicky used to get so cross about Miss Day. 'She makes me so cross. All those terrible purple cardigans. What sort of self-image has she got? Why won't she assert herself? Poor Miss Day!'*

I never agreed with Nicky about Miss Day. Miss Day did some good things, e.g.:

Readers[3] shelves.

A Squires kid was tugging his thing through his trousers and crying onto Miss Day's cardigan.

But he smiled[4] a moment later when she brrmed out backwards from under Easy Readers, with his missing plastic lorry.

'Fanks Iss Ay!' the Squires kid said, snatching his toy back. 'Ayo, Hoolyann Handle.'[5]

Miss Day tugged at a black clump of bubble gum stuck in her purple cardigan. 'We going to win this afternoon then, Julian?'

'Course not.'[6]

Natalie and Co. yaffled behind Pets Corner. And so did our Eliza.

I did not listen to them.

- *she pretended to be a United supporter,*
- *she ran a club in the holidays,*
- *she always knew your name and*
- *ages ago, when I'd had that trouble with my green trousers in the Infants she'd found me three safety pins and never said anything about it ever again, even to me.*

[3] *Those stories in big little words about posh kids who all have dogs and cars and two parents each and happy endings . . . No wonder things are easy, if you get what you want like that.*

[4] *and tugged his thing.*

[5] *Julian Chandler.*

[6] *I didn't even know who we were playing.*

Miss Day said, 'Feeling rough, Julian?'

'Yes.'

'Have a rough biscuit to go with it.' She scooped inside the pocket in her long purple cardigan. 'But turn your back so Mrs Beacon can't see.'

I turned. The biscuit tasted of woolly ginger.

Eliza brought Natalie Thingy over, hand-in-hand. 'Hello, Miss Day. Natalie is my new friend, Miss Day.'

'Julian Chandler's in my class at school, Miss Day,' Natalie yaffled. 'He wets the bed because his mother's run off.'

'Don't.'

'Eliza says, don't you Eliza?'

'Yes Julian and Natalie's my friend.'

I said, 'She knows what she can do. She can – '

'Can't.'

'She can – ' And this time I said it.

Natalie gasped. 'You're not allowed to say that to girls, Julian Chandler!'

'And anyway my mother has *not* run off, because we talk to her on the phone, don't we Eliza?'

'Yes Natalie.'

I nodded. 'See? She's gone round the world actually.'

But Eliza went on, 'It's only pretends when we talk to her, isn't it Julian?'

Natalie yaffled.

I said, 'Why am I in the Children's Library

looking up the Encyclopaedia about the time zones in different parts of the world then?'

Natalie stared.

I nodded. 'And that's what I *am* doing if you'll excuse me. And you Eliza had better be careful what you say to some people.'

'I've been asking her about Chester Julian Chandler and that girl friend you are reckoned to have there and she says you never – '

But I was at Reference by then, squashed at the plastic table and opening the index of the big Encyclopaedia.

I couldn't read it, though. The last time I'd been to this library with Nicky had been in July, just after she forgot my birthday. She'd had a real swearing row with Mrs Beacon that morning, and then taken me on to the fair. And had another row with the man, till she was allowed to take me into the tunnel of love free, because she said it didn't cost them any more electricity whether there was one or two, and I was too young for love, wasn't I, so why should she pay for it? She was brilliant at rows, Nicky, and –

'Hello,' Debbie Henderson said, suddenly in front of me.

'Hello yourself.'

'Why you crying Julian?'

'Not,' I lied.

Debbie Henderson had the darkest eyes in all our school. They were nearly as black as her hair which was nearly as black and shiny as a spaniel's. I loved spaniels . . . Last Christmas Debbie Henderson sent me a letter in our school Christmas post. I posted one back. But then Mr Fever was forced to cancel the school post because some juniors were sending rude messages with very very rude pictures, and my letter had been cancelled too . . .

Debbie's letter, signed 'An amdirer', went:

'Dear Julian Happy Christmas to my boy friend. Please kiss me again. An amdirer.'[7]

I knew some things about Debbie Henderson, e.g. she didn't have a dad, her art work often went up in displays, she liked doing aerobics, her games bag was green and yellow, her sister Gloria had the same black hair only longer, and she went to a school for naughty girls. Debbie was really

[7] *I had never kissed Debbie Henderson actually, but I'd been kissed by Natalie Thingy, and Georgie Donaldson, when there was that craze for kiss-catch.*

But Debbie had only invited two boys to her birthday party – me and Eric Rickaby, and she couldn't have fancied him. In Mrs Harris's when we did country dancing Debbie chose me three times. And at farmers-in-the-dell.

Deborah Jane, she liked chocolate and once had a rabbit but something had eaten it, bones and all, and she thought it might have been Gloria's naughty school friends.

This morning Debbie was wearing pale blue jeans and white socks with her big toes nearly out of them, because she had left her muddy shoes at the door like you should, and we hadn't. She plomped on the carpet. 'What you doing, you?'

I explained about time zones.

'Interesting, that,' she said.

I explained about the Beaufort Wind Scale.

'Interesting, that.'

'Mr Hills told me the day I smashed his tea cup.'

'And his saucer,' she said. 'Mr Hills told us to be nice to you.'

'He didn't.'

'He did, one morning when you were late.'

'I'm always late.'

'That's cos your mum's run off.'

'She's going round the world.'

She said, 'When my dad ran off, he said he was going to make us a room in his new house and we could choose and go and live with him instead of my mother but –'

I turned a page in the index.

She went on, 'I haven't seen him for three years. My mum's stopped crying. And we're on benefits.'

'Well *my* mother's coming home for Christmas. Which is why my father's come in to change her library books today, actually.'

'It makes you disturbed when your parents split up,' Debbie said. 'That's why our Gloria's in the naughty girls' school.'

I turned a page in the index.

She stared. 'You've *got* a girl friend haven't you?'

'Yes. In Chester.'

'Thought so.' She stood up. 'Only there's this girl . . . still that's her hard luck isn't it?'

'Mm?' I mmmed, feeling the blushing come.

She didn't say about that. She pointed over at Eliza. 'Have you heard what your Eliza's asking Miss Day?'

'No?'

'She's asking her to come and live with you and be your new mother.'

I dropped the Encyclopaedia on my thumb, and looked.

It looked true.

Eliza was holding Miss Day's hand and saying, 'There is room at our house. And you *are* a miss aren't you? So will you, plea–'

I saved the day.[8] 'Eliza, you stop hassling Miss Day and come here at once.'

[8] *And the Day*.

37

And she came.[9] I was strangling her gently, just as my father clattered in with the buggy with the frozen shopping and Madge. He drove straight at the Autumn display. Acorns bonged onto Madge, as she tipped forward. He tried to scoop her up, but the buggy was smacking backwards now of course. The milk bottle leaped out of his pocket, cracked itself on the buggy handles, and splodged milk and broken glass from Autumn to Pets.

Mrs Beacon turned. Natalie yaffled, and Miss Day whispered, 'We might lose today, Julian. But you just wait till later in the season.'

That night I was sprawling on the front room floor, wrapped up in the rug Nicky used to take in her canary car for us to spill on. My father came in with a glass of beer.

'Want a sip of the froth Julian?'

'No.'

'Not much of a day was it?'

'No.'

'I'm not sure I can cope without your mother you know?'

'No.' I peered round him so I could still see the telly.

He stood for a bit, and then went back to doing whatever he'd been doing before.

[9] *(!)*

38

7   The Kidnappers

The last week in October, Grandma and Grandad came down from Scotland as usual. I helped wheel in their seven identical suitcases, as usual, and asked Grandad what was happening.

'Och!' he oched. 'It's the traffic, on the low road to England, ye sassenach.' He rubbed my head with his fist, like he always did.

'No, I mean what's happened to Nick–'

But he was already letting the girls ambush him and turn him into a donkey.

I caught Grandma alone in the kitchen, wearing her sunflowery apron.

I asked her what was happening.

'How *is* Grandma's big boy?' She smothered me in sunflowers.

'Smothered,' I said. 'But where's Nick–'

She fumbled in the sunflowers for a glassy mint.[1] 'Don't tell your Grandad.' She poked one

[1] *I don't like glassy mints.*

into my mouth and one into hers.

'Thanks Grandma but do you know where
Nic–'

'We don't speak with our mouths full dear, do
we?'

By the time our mouths weren't full, she was in
the garden dusting the fence and talking rhubarb
with Mrs Embleton.

There was no time for me to ask anything during
all the usual Grandad-and-Grandma presents, tea,
baths, stories, drinks, nappies, songs, shsshs,
tears, prayers[2] etc.

I waited till much later when Grandad sneaked
in as usual, to sit on my bed and talk for hours.
This time he didn't sit.

'If you're a good wee boy I'll wear my kilt
tomorrow and then we'll see what the neighbours
say about.' He always said that.

'Grandma won't let you. But please tell me
where you think Nick–'

'Your Grandma's a terrible woman. But don't tell
her I said so or I'll be – '

[2] *Nicky caught her once and said if it ever happened again*
we wouldn't have any grandparents. Grandma only
whispered prayers after that, and she told me you can
just think them if you have to.

And he'd gone before he could say what he would be.

I did tell her, when she sneaked in even later.
   'God bless, Julian.'
   'Aren't you going to sit down and talk tonight?'
   'Too much to do dear.'
   'Just tell me where Nicky's *gone*?'
   But she'd gone too.

I slept for just long enough to start a dream about the Squireses kids setting fire to Mrs Embleton's rhubarb and blaming Ooolychander[3] while Grandma was downstairs in the kitchen talking about me.
   I woke up, and Grandma still was.
   ' – ulia . . . ig boy . . . ut gir . . .'
   I crept onto the landing to listen.
   '. . . ot as youn . . . acrifices must . . .'
   I crept half downstairs.
   '. . . the children are what mat . . .'
   I crept into the hall, and she was still talking.
   '. . . ouble is that you simply can't manage on your own Jonathan . . .'
   I crept to the kitchen door.
   '. . . so that's what Grandad and I want to do,

[3] *Julian Chandler*.

Jonathan and we won't take no for an answer. We are the grandparents and we have a duty . . .'

Won't take no for an answer.

I knew what Grandma was talking about now.

Grandma and Grandad had come to kidnap us!!!!![4]

I crept back under my duvet with Chonk and we trembled together thinking out a plan to save the family.

It came at five past five a.m.[5]

I crept into Eliza's bed to tell her it. I don't think she had wet herself, for once.

'Awake?'

'Mmmmmmm,' she mmmmed.

'I've got a plan to stop Grandma's plan to kidnap us and she won't take no for an answer and we are a duty so it's the only way. What we've got to do all this weekend is behave as b–'

'Grandma says we *are* allowed to say good night to God.'

I said, 'Nicky says there isn't such a thing as God but the idea me and Chonk have come up with is that we all behave as badl–'

She was asleep again before I'd told her.

[4] *Mr Hills says don't use underlining or italics or exclamation marks, if you can help it.*
    I can't!!!
[5] *Oddly, Madge wasn't head-cracking.*

Before breakfast I rang up Debbie Henderson to see if she could help.

3 5 6 4 7 3[6][7]

When she answered, I said, 'You know when your parent ran off and your naughty sister Gloria turned naughty and had to go to the naughty girls' school?'

'I *am* her sister Gloria who turned naughty, who are you?'

'Julian Ch–,' I said. I should just have put the phone down of course. Or said she was a wrong number. Or –

'And anyway, how do you know about my dad running off and me going to the naughty girls' school, Julian Ch?'

'I've rung the wrong num–'

'The naughty girls' school's flooded this weekend because someone naughty left all the taps on. Our Debbie's still in bed. What do you want?'

'Ask her something.'

'What?'

'Can't remember.'

'When boys ring me up I tell them they're

---

[6] *Not her real number of course, I don't want everyone ringing her.*

[7] *But I rang her real number of course.*

43

dumped because you have to or they dump you, Julian Ch.'

'I'm Jamie Learmouth really, I was just pretending to be Julian Ch.'

'Our Debbie was talking about a Julian last night. His mother's run off, like our dad did.'

'She hasn't.'

'And *his* dad's got a new blonde girl friend[8] instead.'

'Whose dad's?'

'Yours.'

'There's someone knocking at our door,' I lied, knocking on the table. I smacked the phone down, and blushed like the baboon's bum.[9]

Then I muddled up the breakfast cutlery, mixed up the cereals, fingered some wax out of my ear and

[8] *Again?!*
[9] *Mr Hills says when we write stories we aren't allowed to just write the first thing that comes into our head, e.g. green as grass and white as snow. We have to struggle with the words and be fresh, e.g. we can't say nice or thing . . .*
Baboons.
Baboons live in Africa. They have long tails. But when you look under them, they are bald and red.

dropped it in the milk jug.[10] I unscrewed the salt cellar, and put the top back loose.

I'd just finished clawing two paw marks in the butter, when Grandma cuddled the girls into breakfast and said what lovely dresses they had, and they would have to be very careful not to spill, wouldn't they?

I said they could spill if they wanted.

Grandma said, 'I really think perhaps it would be nice if you didn't have breakfast half-dressed Julian?'

'Nice isn't fresh.'

'You should at least have something on your feet? And please take them off the table?'

'I live here,' I babooned.

She said, 'We were hoping to have a nice breakfast all together. We don't really want to see your feet.'

'Better than *your* feet,' I said. 'You've got verrucas.'

She sat the girls down, napkinned them and brought her usual banquet of bacon, sausage, tomatoes, eggs, mushrooms, fried bread and toast.

I started singing.

Eliza joined in.

Grandma had asked us to stop three times.

'I like singing,' I sang.

[10] *A jug for milk? At Number 77!!!!????????????????*

45

Grandma said, 'But not when you're eating, so eat up like good boys and girls.'

I slithered my plate across the table.

'Not good are we, Eliza?'

'No, Grandma,' Eliza said. 'We wee the bed.'

Grandma slid my plate back. 'All the more important to get some good food inside you now.'

'Your breakfast's not good. There's a waxy thing in the milk and the cat's been in the butter. And anyway in this family we're not allowed to eat dead pigs.'

I tiddleywinked my plate. A sausage flew into my pajama lap.

It smelt lovely.

Grandma said, 'Eat up Eliza. Julian's just in one of his moods.'

I said, 'Eliza doesn't eat dead pig because our mother says not to, doesn't she Eliza?'

'She does, Grandma.'

'My mother decides what happens in this house. We don't believe in pigs or God or Grandmas who come here interfering.' I tiddleywinked Eliza's breakfast up the wall.

Grandma went for Grandad.

I said to Eliza, 'Put salt in your drink, it's very good for you.'

She did, and the salt top came off.

Grandad came in with tissue paper on his

shaved face. 'Och, and what's exactly going on here?'

I said, 'Eliza told me to tip the breakfasts over. She's in one of her moods isn't she Grandma?'

Eliza stared.

I said, 'And she's put all the salt in her drink, on purpose.'

Eliza smacked Madge.

Grandma picked up Madge, who tried to bite her. Grandad picked up Eliza, forgot how heavy she'd got, and dropped her in the marmalade. Chonk volleyed onto the table and pinched the bacon.

I splashed milk into my glass. 'It's always like this here. We're dead disturbed. Nobody'd want to live with us.'

I guzzled the whole glassful of milk in one noisy slurp. And then remembered – the waxy thing.

After I'd been sick, I squeezed toothpaste all over the bathroom mirror. When Grandma came in to load the washing machine I swore in the word my father had used the night the phone rang and it wasn't Nicky.

'Don't talk like that Julian dear.'

'What did I say?'

'Swearing's a sign of a poor vocabulary dear.'

'What's vocabulary supposed to be?'

'All the wonderful words there are in the

English language and – '

'Swearing's words in the English language.'

'Some words are not nice for – ' She saw the toothpaste.

I said, 'Nice isn't nice. And Nicky swears. So *you* can't have been good parents. And I can swear as much as I want.' And I did.

She said, 'Please stop, dear.'

I closed my eyes and chanted all the swear words I knew till she hit me.

But all she did was start wiping off the toothpaste, and humming.

I squirted tomato sauce up her sleeve when we had a pub lunch in Bakewell, I fell in the river when we had a walk in Bakewell, and I used all the hot water when we had to come home early from Bakewell.

I boiled in our bath and thought of 101 new ways of stopping the kidnap.[11]

[11] *e.g. flooding the floor; crunching biscuits in Eliza's bed; pinching the telly tuning thing so they'd have to watch Channel Four all night; wetting the bed; walking round half-dressed; having nightmares; singing offensive songs all night; switching lights on and off; ringing the speaking clock and then saying Eliza said Grandma was wanted for an emergency message; using all the hot water and not letting anybody in, however desperate.*

Then I wandered about in just my pajama bottoms, tipped Grandma's handbag into the fireplace in the back room, wasted a whole big box of matches Grandad had bought specially for the cooker and sang my new version of the song Jamie Learmouth said his brother had made up.[12]

> The night was dark and stormy
> The lavvy light was dim
> The last thing we heard Grandma shout
> Was 'O dear I've fallen in'.

And that was when my father sent me up to bed, at three minutes to six p.m.[13]

I kissed Nicky, and explained how my idea to save the family was working so far. But she wouldn't look at me, so I put her back behind the Beanos, and sat up in bed to sing all night.

The night was dark and stormy
The –

But thoughts kept coming . . . What would Gloria tell Debbie? . . . How had the cub football gone today without me? . . . Who was this new blonde girl friend? . . . Where *was* Nicky? Why hadn't she been able to write to us or ring us up or . . .

[12] *He never had.*
[13] *This will be in the next Guinness Book of Records.*

The last thing I remember was wetting the bed
and thinking how hot it was, how it went on
spreading, how naughty I was and how . . .

I woke up at ten to midnight smelling like the fish
pier at Scarborough last summer. We'd all still been
happy then. The only things in the world I'd
wanted were a dog, a brother, and my place back
in the cub football team. But now –

I sang, then screamed. Nobody took any notice.
So I banged downstairs whistling. Grandma and
Grandad were sipping whisky in front of the telly,
that was on too loud.

'What do you want *now*?'

'Nothing, Grandma. Cos I want doesn't get.'

'Then I would suggest you put on some dry
pajamas and go back to bed, Julian.'

'Suggest what you want . . . Where's he then?'

'Your father . . . has gone out.'

'He never goes out.'

'Then perhaps it's a good thing we are here now
so he can.'

'Who's he gone out with then?'

Grandad nudged me with his whisky glass. 'Sit
here next to me and let's have a little chat, laddie.'

'No.'

'Yes.' He tugged me onto the sofa so he could
cuddle me next to him. And he kept me cuddled
there too. 'You're shivering you poor sassenach.'

Grandma said, 'Your behaviour today Julian has been quite appall–'

Grandad said, 'Sshshs Grandma, remember what we agreed?'

I said, 'What did you agr–'

Grandad cuddled me harder. 'Shhsh, you. It's all right.'

'It isn't! . . . My mother got up one morning and went round the world and she never even bothered telling me and now you're all pretending she never even *existed*.'

They were actually listening! So I went on. 'It's like Mrs Embleton said. When Mr Embleton died no one talked to her about him, cos they thought it would remind her he was dead all over again. As if she'll ever forget. MY MOTHER'S GONE!'

She said, 'Your behaviour today doesn't help.'

'We're *disturbed*! We wet the beds and have nightmares and scream. It was all bad enough before, but now you've come to break up what's left of our family and – kidnap us.'

'Kidnap you?' Grandad said.

'I heard you in the kitchen last night. You want to take us kids off to Scotland.'

Grandma even turned off the telly. 'We love the three of you very much indeed, Julian. But – Grandad and I couldn't possibly look after another family at our age . . .' She smiled a little sad smile.

He smiled too. 'No. Only in the very worst

circumstances if your father really – '

'Really couldn't cope,' she said.

I said, 'So why aren't you going to take no for an answer then?'

'What we *are* going to do is help where we can.'

Grandad rubbed my head. 'Financial help. However proud your father might be – '

And then she said something really surprising. 'We think your father is doing remarkably well in a situation that's remarkably hard for him.'

I stared. The world was stopping making sense. I'd always thought she thought my father was useless too. Whenever she was in the house she –

But that wasn't my real problem.

My problem was that my plan to stop being kidnapped had turned out to be exactly the wrong way round.

I said, 'You mean, it's only if we get *really* out of control and disturbed that you'd take us off to Scotland?'

They nodded.

'So really,' I said, 'the better we behave and the happier we are the more likely we are *not* to be kidnapped?'

They nodded again.

I said, 'I don't think I am *very* disturbed really, actually.'

They shook.

'I'm probably just sickening for something?'

'Beddybyes then,' Grandma said. 'Some nice clean jimjams.'

She led me hand-in-hand upstairs, remade my bed and found a glassy mint.

'Grandma, I'm not disturbed – '

'Of course you're not, you're a big brave boy.'

'Yes, but please just tell me where N– '[14]

'Not with your mouth full dear.'

I slept a long dry night, woke up tasting of broken glass and ran in to warn Eliza and Madge to behave themselves today. But they were already breakfasting. I dressed, washed, combed and went downstairs to try to be nice all day.

And was.[15]

[14] ' –icky is. And where my father's gone out to? Who with? And who is this new blonde girl friend?'
       And who was the old one?

[15] e.g.:
       • I told Grandad it didn't matter that United had lost again because it was the game that mattered;

I did manage one bit of real talk with Grandad, while we played the longest snooker game in the world.

'You know Nicky, Grandad?'

'Not very well.'

'What do you mean?'

'Nicky surprises people. No doubt she'll surprise us again, soon.'

'What's really going on, Grandad?'

'I'm trying to play this shot.'

'. . . You aren't.'

They set off on the low road to Scotland at exactly five o'clock, as usual.

- *I helped the girls make Thank You cards;*
- *I took my father tea in bed and made sure everyone heard me saying I hoped he had had a good night out with whoever he was with;*
- *I said Grandma's hair looked very nice and not at all dyed. She said it wasn't dyed and who had said it was?*
- *I didn't tell her (it was Nicky);*
- *I let Grandad beat me at snooker, even though he was trying to let* me *beat* him. *Our one frame took two hours, and he had to let himself win in the end or they wouldn't have been able to go home.*

We'd not been kidnapped.

My father sang as he bathed the girls. I didn't ask him why. Nobody gave me a proper answer. And they didn't seem to know it themselves.

8   Men Always Shrug

The next good thing was Auntie Marion.

She wasn't really an auntie.[1]

My father went back to shiny trousers, aftershaves and the building society. And Auntie Marion came to look after us.

Life at Number 77 became normal again.

In fact it became more normal than when it was normal. The towels stopped smelling. The socks started coming back in pairs. There was soap again, and toothpaste, loo paper, beans, biscuits, bulbs, and eggs. And the stove started staying in.

And I stopped being late for school.

That was because Auntie Marion said I was a big boy now and old enough to go on my own, like I'd been saying since when I wasn't. My father said

[1] *She was probably someone else's auntie of course. She lived round the corner, on the estate, and she'd looked after us when Madge was being born. We liked her already but she did squodge.*

what about the main road. Auntie Marion said there was a lollipop lady. My father said he had never seen a lollipop lady there. I said that was because we were always late. He said in that case how did *I* know there was a lollipop lady. Auntie Marion said she knew because the lollipop lady was her sister. Eliza said she liked lollipops.

Auntie Marion won. My father agreed that I could go to school on my own, so long as it would be my fault when I was run over.

I wasn't. But now I was a big boy, I could pop in to see people on the way home.

I popped in to see Nicky's pal Sandy.

Now, most of Nicky's pals lived in London or the middle of town in big houses with posters and blinds and garlic and smoke. But she did have this one friend Sandy who lived opposite the Co-op, and stuck Women's posters on her trees.

It was four o'clock in the middle of my second week as a big boy when I popped. She answered the door wearing her mucky red dressing gown, showing her mucky feet with red toenails. She shouted, 'Clear off. We don't believe in Trick or Treat because it's typical stupid American blackmail and – I know you?'

'I'm Nicky's son. You did Women's Only yoga[2] with her.'

She waved me into the kitchen, full of garlic and smoke. There was a huge Greenpeace whale on one wall, and a huge red woman breaking chains on another. There was a blackboard with a rude message, and a pin board with greasy newspaper cuttings. We used to have just the same garlic, smoke, posters and cuttings at our house, till Auntie Marion came.

Sandy filled herself a mug of white wine from a giant green bottle, and asked me what I drank.

'Nothing thank you.' The crockery was even dirtier than it used to be at our house.

'Carrot and yoghurt cake?' she offered.

'No thank you.'

'Don't blame you.' She sat on the table edge and dangled her legs. 'What *do* you want then?'

She tugged her dressing gown round her.

I blushed. 'Nicky's gone.'

'Where?'

'I don't know. Do you?'

[2] *An Eastern method of getting Awareness with exercises. 'Yoga' is a Sanskrit word. Nothing to do with yoghurt, yogurt or hotyog.*

   A yogi is good at yoga (except Yogi Bear, as far as I am Aware).

'I'd have to say I didn't even if I did, Julian. Women are sisters you see.'

'I only want to write to her.'

'I don't know where she is.'

'But you'd say that – even if you did?'

'Yes but I really don't.'

'You'd say that too.'

'Yup.' She sipped her wine.

I stared at the threatened whale hoping it felt sorry for me. 'She's gone round the world.'

'Good for her.'

'It's not good for us.'

She leaned forward and put her arms round my neck. I blushed and mumbled into her red dressing gown and skin. 'Do you think she really can have gone round the world?'

'Women can do anything.'

I stared at the woman breaking the chains.

Sandy said, 'I've worked at two women's refuges where women hide from the husbands who batter them.'

'My father never battered anyone.'

'Sure?'

'Even us.'

'Men have other ways of dominating their women.'

'*She* dominated *him* if – '[3]

[3] '– *dominated means what I think*' (it did).

'So who did the washing up at your house? And who went to the football matches? Whose car was it? Who – '

'He hates football, and he always wash–'

'You interrupted, Julian, and just because you're a Man you think you can.'

'I can't and – I don't think I'm a man.'

'Won't be long though will it?' But she squeezed me again. 'So why's she gone?'

'That's what I came to ask you.' I shrugged.

'Shrugging won't help. Men always shrug when you come to an emotional problem. You won't *grow*.'

She lifted me onto the table to dangle, and *I* dangled as she walked round her kitchen sipping wine and talking . . .[4]

[4] *e.g:*

Men are like children, she said, but they are in charge everywhere.

Take my school, for example, with a Man head teacher and a Man caretaker?

Why did the Women in my school do the cooking and the typing? Why weren't there proper places for Women to feed babies and leave their children?

Who did all the interrupting?

Who drove the cars and drank the beer and talked about football and how awful Women are?

Who started all the wars?

Who stared at photographs of naked Women in their newspapers to humiliate their wives and daughters etc.?

Then she gargled white wine, and said, 'You don't understand a word I'm saying do you Julian?'

'I do . . . Nicky used to say it and anyway we don't look at naked women at our house.' I blushed. 'And my father doesn't drive a c–.'

'Is that the time?' She looked at the kitchen clock and swore, nearly as well as Nicky. 'I'm supposed to be doing a meeting.'

'Please, Sandy, *if* you find out where she is even if you don't know now – ?'

'If I do find out I'll not tell you, right?' She went out and came back in wearing jeans and pullover before I'd even got off the table. 'But if I *don't* find out, I *will* tell you, right?' She squeezed me again. 'Come on, I'll drive you home chop chop.'

She had a grey B Reg Peugeot 205 with so many stickers in the back she couldn't see out. 'Hold on to that door, it's wonky, where men keep driving into it.'

She drove like Nicky, very fast in second gear, and shouted at the men drivers even when they were women. She parked in the middle of the road outside the minimarket, and ran out, in, out, for a packet of rolling tobacco and an onion bhaji.

'Eat it. You can get home on your own from here?'

'Course. I'm a big boy.'

'You all are.'

'Thanks for the lift,' I said, trying to shut her

wonky door. I was further from home now than I had been at school.

She called, 'And you try thinking what it feels like from inside other people. It's the only way we can ever understand each other. But Men aren't very good at feelings are you?'

She squodged her gears and nearly hit a 45 bus. Driven by a woman, I think.

I waved, wondering why I felt happier, and why I liked her so much, and why I wanted her to like me.

I threw the onion bhaji over the vicar's hedge and jogged home.

That Friday night I was in my room trying to make my computer work.[5]

My father shouted upstairs, 'Someone on the phone for you . . . Come on, it's someone important.'

I went down slowly. I was a big boy now, even if my mother was on the phone to tell us she loved us and was on her way home.

But she wasn't.

It was Baloo from the cubs. 'Hello there, Julian! Tomorrow morning? Not doing anything are you?

[5] *Nicky used to do the plugs.*

Play for us?[6] Ten o'clock at the library?[7] You still there Julian?'

'I'm not initiated.'

'This flu bug's jiggered us. But it'll reflect badly on the whole troop if we can't turn out tomorrow.'

'My mum might be coming home tomorrow, Baloo.'

'Be finished by midday.' And then, when I didn't say anything he said, 'Young Jamie says you were cross we had to drop you. It's what football's about I'm afraid. But with the bug and this business with your mother, he thought we could do you a good turn.'

[6] *I played eleven matches last season, striker and defender. Then I was suddenly dropped because five Beavers had gone up. I was suddenly just a spectator, blushing in my shorts and a teeshirt because Jamie Learmouth said I had to give the shirt back. They lost 20-something nil. I stayed at home after that, waiting for my recall to the squad.*

If things had been different, I might have got initiated in the cubs actually. I liked their badges, and their assault course at Walesby where you can break your arms if you want.

[7] *Nicky used to say the said cubs were ridiculous. Boys pretending to be men, tying themselves up in knots, playing at soldiers and pretending they didn't need women. But who washed their uniforms after?*

'He thought wrong.'

'You won't play?'

'Can't.'

He began to talk about Baden-Powell and no-such-word-as-can't.

I said, 'I can't hear you because there's someone at the door.' And I put the phone down.

My father came in with a can of beer.

'Who was it?'

'Baloo. I've got my place back in the football team tomorrow.'

'What time?'

'Ten o'clock . . . I'm not going.'

'Oh.'

'That you, young Julian?'

Mrs Embleton caught me at the end of our road, scuffing my shoes, the Tuesday after[8], and I had to shuffle home with her.

'I've been going through my Christmas card list, young Julian.'

'It's not even November yet, Mrs Embleton.'

'It might not be even November yet for some people, but some people don't like to do everything in a mad rush.'

'No,' I said, and then, 'Yes.' Five houses further on I said, 'I'm more of a mad rush person myself.'

[8] *The cubs had lost on Saturday to St John's 0-14.*

'Well you slow down then. I am a senior citizen not a gazelle.'[9] We slowed down. 'My worry is I just don't know where to send your mother's Christmas card.'

'She'll be home on December the 11th, so you can give it her then.'

Three more houses and a lamp-post further on she said, 'I like helping the Scouts with the Scout post.'

'The Scouts are ridiculous, tying themselves in knots, and then getting their mothers to wash their uniforms.'

'Yes, and where's *your* mother? You told me she was in Doncaster at a glove factory but there isn't a glove factory in Doncaster, I asked my home help.'

'There isn't now because she led a strike.'

'Poor Mr Embleton took me to Doncaster once for the races and we had butterscotch all day.'

And she told me (again).

Remembering it made her cry. Perhaps it was the wind too, and being disappointed at not being a gazelle.

[9] *An antelope with light and dark horizontal stripes on face.*

Both sexes have horns.

If ever you are in any doubt about deciding which is gazelle and which senior citizen, Mrs Embleton does not have horns.

I mumbled little ums and mmmmms all the long way home. When we got there she told me I shouldn't scuff my shoes. And she said she was beginning to think something terrible had happened to my mother. Like she'd been *murdered*.[10]

But as it turned out, the next exciting thing wasn't murder. It was what happened to Mr Fever's trousers, on Guy Fawkes Night.

[10] *MURDERED???*

Part Three

9 Trousers In Flames

We got to the bonfire late, so we had to stand miles away. It wouldn't light properly so the Parent Teachers kept fetching petrol, and Mr Fever kept megaphoning everyone to stand well back when he threw it on.

I hung round with my sisters for a bit, in case any kids wanted to be funny about me not bringing my mother but then I went for treacle toffee at Mr Hills's table down by the entrance.

As soon as I queued, Natalie Thingy tried to blind me. Jamie Learmouth was with her in his best white jacket with the gold zips.

I said, 'She'll blind somebody, waving her sparkler about like that.'

'Good,' Jamie said. 'And anyway she knows something about your dad, Julie-Anne.'

'Doesn't,' I said.

'Who's *she*? The cat's grandma?' Natalie yaffled.

'Yes,' I said.

'Take no notice whatsoever of *him*, James darling.'[1]

'I won't.'

We queued. He paid for her treacle toffee. She stared at me, then said, 'Anyway, my mum's seen your dad with a blonde[2] woman in his car. So shift.'

She elbowed me and slithered off into the dark with her darling.

'Good night *James* darling!' I called, too late, and not loud enough. 'A quarter of treacle toffee please, Mr Hills?'

'Um, enjoying yourself, Julian?'

'No, Mr Hills. You see I have never understood why people make such a fuss about Guy Fawkes blowing up parliament. It needs it. Guy Fawkes is innocent, OK?'[3]

He poked up in his mouth for a bit of his own bonfire toffee stuck to the roof. 'Don't you tell Mr Um Fever will you? He's very keen on parliaments.'

Madge was crying when I got back to my happy

[1] *James? Darling!!!*
[2] *Again? The same new blonde? Or a new one?*
[3] *I was only saying exactly what Nicky had said last year. It did not seem a year.*

70

family, so I took her over my shoulder for a walk out of the smoke.

My father said, 'Be careful then.'

'I'll be more careful than you, she's my sister and the last one I'm likely to get.'[4]

I tiptoed behind the smoky crowd, and talked to get her calm. 'Remember last year Madge when Nicky pushed us right to the front? You miss Nicky don't you? Well, we *should* miss her. Cos if we forget her she'll know and she'll forget *us*. But if we keep talking about her and crying if we feel we want to, and if we don't try to keep our feelings in and get ill, like Men do, like Sandy says and it's what Nicky told us too, and – '

By now I'd wandered right into the teachers' playground.

I was just about to explain to Madge how Men are no good about feelings and just shrug instead, and there was this girl calling, 'Talking to yourself now are you Julian Chandler?'

'Sshshs, no need to be frightened.'

'Not frightened.'

'Don't mean you. I mean our Madge.'

She wore a woolly balaclava with breath coming out of it. But I knew who she was.[5]

[4] *I still wanted a brother, mind you.*
[5] *Debbie Henderson.*

71

'What you been telephoning our Gloria for?'

'Nothing.'

'Was it about your mother not coming back?'

'Forgot.'

'Your dad's got another woman.'

'Hasn't.'

'Natalie's mum saw him in his car with a blonde.'

'He hasn't got a car.'

'Where *is* your mum then?'

'Our neighbour Mrs Embleton thinks she's been murdered, actually.'

'*Murdered?*'

She whistled. We stood for ages.

The she said, 'Can I have a go of your baby?'

'Be careful then.'

She was, for a bit. Then she said, 'How's your girl friend in Chester?'

'All right.'

'You don't know where Chester is.'[6]

There was a sudden flare up from the fire, and some shouting. We ran back just in time to see that Mr Fever's trousers were in flames, in both legs.

[6] *Do. It's at the top of the Dee estuary. It was called Deva by the Romans. It's 30 miles south of Liverpool. See.*

Eric Rickaby's dad who's a fireman was flinging Mr
Fever onto the grass and lying on him.

Mr Fever was lucky.
But I –

10 Dusky Bluebells

– was rushed home from school a week after,
to die.

My father hoped to save me with the
Encyclopaedia of Total Family Health. He sat on
my legs, hurting, and asked questions as I slipped
in and out of consciousness. Did my head hurt?
Was there a rash on my tummy? What colour was
my tongue? Did my ears gurgle? Did –
   Everything went black outside, which is what it
should as you die, till the lights come on again at
the very end.[1][2]
   I went bang in my head. Hot glue gushed down
my nose, and spurted everywhere, and it was
blood.
   He panicked.

[1] *How does anyone know?*
[2] *Because some people have died then come back from the
     dead, and described their out-of-body experiences.*
          Me for one.

I said, 'If you man hadn't she would still and only son not dying not. And –'

'I can't understand anything you're saying.'

'That's a man you because are you!'

The Doctor told me to stick out my tongue, but I couldn't.

He told me to open my mouth, but it wouldn't.

My father begged the doctor to say I was all right, but I wasn't.

But in the morning there was sunshine, and it was far too bright with bottles dancing in it.

'Those bottles?'

'Your medicine, Julian,' my father said. He looked pale, as if he cared.

'They dancing.'

'They aren't.'

'They singing ten green bottles.'

'They not.'

'Men can't feel.'

I was lying in my coffin, without a lid. It was crammed with dusky bluebells from the top of our garden. Nicky was bending over, waiting with me for my turn to be slotted into the earth, next to the dead pets where I'd not dared go alive but was now going alone, dead for ever.

I could hear the dusky bluebells tinkling purple

in my coffin, under me. The white bulbs were silent and cold on my spine.

Nicky tippytiptapped on my shoulder.

Please, she said, try to hang on till I come home for Christmas but why was the room such a mess, with earth everywhere? Wasn't it time Men woke up to the fact that – ?

I woke up, singing.

'In and out the dusky bluebells
You shall be my partner
Tippy tipp tip tap on my shoulder –

My eyes were still gunged with tears. But I knew for absolute, positive, total, complete certain, that Nicky would be sitting on my bed looking down at me when I opened my eyes and came back.[3]

'Nicky!'

But it was Auntie Marion who answered. 'Drink up, chucky egg.'

'I can smell bluebells.'

'Those wonderful roses on the window ledge, more like.'

[3] *When you are in a coma your parents have to sit on your bed and get pop stars to record messages to wake you up.*
Separated parents get back together while they sit waiting and being sorry.
(I was not *pretending by the way.)*

76

'From Nicky?'
'From me.'

Eliza came in with her stethoscope.

I whispered, 'Nicky came to look at me when I was dead, doctor.'

'I a nurse.'

'You have to be a doctor.'

'Can I be dead when I'm a big girl?'

'Nicky's coming back for Christmas, if we can just hang on.'

'I dead.'

And the morning after that, some shouting voice woke me up from a dream of dreaming, and dying without anyone noticing.

'I'll never catch up! I'll have to pretend for ever I've learned things I haven't and then I'll have to be naughty like Graham Squires so no one knows and I love Debbie Henderson and she'll find somebody else and –'

And I stopped because I suddenly knew who was shouting.[4]

My barefoot father yawned at my door. 'It's half past four in the morning, Julian.'

'I'm going mad,' I said. 'People do, when things go mad. But it isn't mad to go mad when things go

[4] *Me.*

77

mad. It's sane. It's madder to be sane in a mad world. It's saner to be mad . . . I want you to sleep here.'

And he did. I let him have a bit of my duvet.

'I must be mad,' he said, towards dawn.

Two days later he took me walking.

I said I wasn't a gazelle. We slowed down.

I asked, 'What would you be doing at your building society now, if you were at work?'

'Adding things up.'

'What after that?'

'Adding more things up.'

He bought us a pint of beer and a coke and two bags of cheese and onion, and we shivered in the Crown doorway.

'These crisps are like bandages.'

'Your taste's coming back, Julian. You're getting better.'

'People do get better just before they die.'

We crouched in the wind.

He said, 'There was a king once whose last words were about how much he fancied eating a pork pie.'

'I fancy eating a pork pie.'

He bought two and we were allowed in the Crown.

It was all buttoned shiny seats and horse brasses

and cigars and pork pies.

I said, 'Pork pies are pigs whiskers and toe nails.'

'Good.'

'How do you know about kings and pork pies, anyway?'

'We know all kinds of things when we don't have to waste our lives in offices and schools.' He seemed to be saying something important.[5] He nodded. I nodded.

'Did you write to Nicky to tell her I was dying?'

'. . . I don't know where she is.'

We sipped.

I said, into my glass, 'Perhaps she's been murdered.'

'Nicky wouldn't let anyone murder her.'

We sipped.

'I dreamed she came to see me in my coffin.'

'That's a bit morbid, Julian.'

'What's morbid mean?'

'Dreaming of yourself in your own coffin. Or – '

'It was crammed with bluebells. And Nicky said she'll be back for Christmas. It'll be all right, Dad.'

'. . . My own Dad smiled just before *he* died. He'd been remembering a kid he'd been at school

[5] *He was.*
   It's when he first started getting the idea that was going to lead to the next idea that was going to change everything.

79

with seventy-two years before and then . . . everything he remembered just went for ever . . .'

'Well,' I said, 'I don't seem to have died.'

I pointed to my plate, where the pork pie had been.

'That's all right then,' he said.

11 Reindeers On The Roof

Actually Nicky didn't manage to come home by
December the 11th, after her Eighty Days.
Christmas started to come instead.

Eliza's first present was from her Playgroup
teacher. It was a pink party balloon to hang outside
the house[1] and ten pink party invitations,
envelopes and pretend stamps.

  I said she hadn't got ten friends. She started
crying. I said it was a joke, and asked who she was
going to invite?

  'Everybody.'

  'You only invite people you like.'

  'I like everybody.'[2]

[1] *to show people they weren't invited.*

[2] *Nobody liked me. I'd not been to a single party since my
    mother had gone off round the world. Not even to Eric
    Rickaby's, and Eric Rickaby always invited the whole
    class, because nobody liked him. And it was always a
    visit to the fire station, or a video of last year's visit to
    the fire station instead.*

I wrote her invitations in green felt tip in best baboon writing. And she stabbed red kisses on them, licked the envelopes, stamped the pretend stamps, and put them on the pile.

'Who's invitation number ten for?'

'Miss Day at the library.'

We wrote, enveloped, stamped and piled Miss Day.

Then I wrote Eliza a list of games, e.g. musical bumps, dead fishes, passing-the-parcels, apple-bobbing and balloon-between-your-legs and Postman's Knock. And of course in-and-out-the-dusky-bluebells.

We pretended the games, then eating the gunge for tea, then getting stomach-pumped in hospital. I said she had to be the doctor because Nicky wouldn't let her be just a nurse. She cried, so to cheer her up I showed her the secret photo.

'Me!' she said.

'Nicky.'

She kissed the photograph, and borrowed it for the night . . .

We didn't think about the ten pink party invitations again, till miles after Christmas.

Before Christmas there were:

1 Three hours of carol concert. Most parents left during Mr Fever's closing speech about the real meaning of Christmas, because

     nobody could hear him because he was
     hidden by Mrs Hanns's oxen and asses.
2 Jenny Holmes's fainting when the Infants
     dropped baby Lord Jesus on his head.
3 Debbie Henderson's giving me a card on
     lined paper and saying, 'Don't read it now,
     daft. It's for Christmas.'
     'Thought it might be.'

I walked home in the dark of the darkest day
there ever is,[3] singing like a big boy, to stop
myself reading her card till I reached the railway
bridge just as the Manchester train clattered
underneath.

    'Merry Xmas and a prosprous new Year. Hope
    your mum comes home from Deborah
    (Henderson).'[4]

And there was a cross that might have been
a kiss.

I danced home like a gazelle. Mrs Embleton was
standing on our steps bottom in her fuzzy slippers.
I nearly knocked her over.
   'Out gathering winter fuel Mrs Embleton?'

[3] *December 21st.*
[4] *So not just an amdirer this year! Her handwriting had*
    changed too.

83

'That you young Julian? The Boy Scouts have let me down.'

'I'm not surprised. They're macho, militaristic, chauv–'

'I don't know how I'm supposed to get this card to your mother now.'

'She'll be here for Christmas.'

'It *is* Christmas.'

'I thought you thought she'd been murdered anyway?'

'Take no notice. I'm always whittling. Here, you have it.'

I showed Dad Mrs Embleton's card. He smelt of chewing gum and said that most people *were* nice really.

I said nice isn't a nice word.

He said, 'Nice *is* nice. It's very nice. How can nice not be nice if nice is nice? It's so nice you have to smile when you say nice.' He smiled. 'Nice.'

I said had he been drinking.

He said it was Christmas and time to put up the tree.

'Do you know where it is?' I asked.

'Nope.'

'Men never do know where things are in their own homes. And when they do any work round the home they get it wrong on purpose so that the Women do it next time and –'

'Know who you sound like? Your mother is who you sound like.' He smiled.

'That's nice,' I said.

It took him till quarter to twelve to find the tree, on top of their wardrobe, with two years' dust on it.[5]

I told him what Women thought was wrong with Christmas and how Men have to try to *feel* but men aren't very good at it.

He shrugged. 'You'll be a man too.'

'Can't help that.'

He smiled. 'Have some froth, then. Pretend it's Christmas.'

Grandma and Grandad came on the 23rd as usual. Grandad said 'Och' and Grandma did all the decorations again.

Eliza couldn't sleep on Christmas Eve, even after I'd hypnotized her.

'What if Father Christmas doesn't come, Julian?'

'He will.'

'Promise.'

[5] *We didn't have Christmas last year. Nicky had decided it celebrated the wrong things – e.g. a male baby born to a male god, worshipped by male shepherds and male kings, while a fat male with a beard rode about in his vehicle, and the Women stayed at home cooking.*

85

'I don't have to promise. He's true.'

'For ever?'

'Yes,' I lied. 'And Nicky's coming home for Christmas as well.'

'For ever and ever?'

'Yes.'

She slept then, and I went back to my own bed to listen to the bells through the wall donging midnight on Mrs Embleton's telly.[6]

I wondered how far Nicky had got.

But there was no hurry. There were twelve days of Christmas for her to choose from.

She'd come.

And surprise us.

I'd not even think about her till she did, because she wouldn't be a surprise if I was expecting her.

And at about three o'clock I rolled on my back listening to the scrabbling reindeers on our roof, and slept for half an hour.

[6] *At midnight on Christmas Eve, Mr Hills told us, all the animals in the world kneel down. But only when nobody is watching. I wondered how anyone could ever* know, *if they couldn't be watched. Or if it was only when the cows and oxen* thought *they weren't being watched . . .?*

I also wondered how far the Wise Men had got by midnight? And if the Shepherds had set off yet? And why they didn't all bump into Father Christmas? And . . .

12   Twelve Days Of Our Christmas

On the 1st Day of our Christmas:
1   Madge got a box of very tiny books about a
    monkey.
2   Eliza got a baby cassette player with big
    switches that she could never break.[1]
3   I didn't get a dog.[2]
4   But I did get:

> The Complete Boys'[3] Conjuring
> Not Recommended For Children Under Five
> Made in Korea How to AMAZE Your Friends
> With Easy To Follow Instructions.

There was a picture on the lid, of a four-year-old
Korean conjuror AMAZING his friends. He looked
like the Squireses.

[1] *It broke on Boxing Day.*
[2] *I want doesn't.*
[3] *Q: Who's an incomplete boy?*
    A: Me.

The Easy To Follow Instructions weren't, The Disappearing Ace wouldn't. But I did AMAZE Eliza by slicing off her head with the Chicago Magic Knife.

The NEWS said there were no trains all day.

On the 2nd day of our Christmas, United lost 4-1, Grandma got wobbly, said it wasn't her sherry trifle, and went to bed for five hours.

The NEWS said there were a few trains running a skeleton service.[4]

Very early on the 3rd day, I tiptoed into the kitchen to see if anyone had come by surprise in the night, and to eat sherry trifle if they hadn't.

I found my father AMAZING himself in front of a mirror.

He waved me to sit. 'Ladies and Jellyspoons! Bees and Gulls! Nothing up my sleeve except my arm. No wires or strings – thus. Now I want you to examine this Ace of Spades. Thank you.'

'Shhhhm – mine,' I said slurping sherry trifle from the fridge before Grandma got up and bust me.

'Absolute concentration please! Drrrrrrrrrr. Thish! Tong!!!'

[4] *Ghost trains? Ha ha.*

'Shin your other hand.'

'Course.' He held out his other hand. 'Oh?' It was empty.

'AMAZING!' I yawned. 'You been up all night practising that?'

'Yes.'

On the 4th day, Grandma said we had to put on sturdy shoes because she had not breathed since Scotland.

Eliza cried because there was going to be a real train with real smoke on television, and she wanted to see it. I lent her my World Snooker video to video over, and we all went out to breathe. Grandma got dog muck in the hollow bits of her sturdy shoes, and said dogs shouldn't be allowed. I did not agree.

Then we all picnicked, in our pajamas, in the front room, on turkey and jelly. And we watched Eliza's video of the real train with the real smoke that turned out to be – The Railway Children.[5]

Now, I knew these Railway Children. They're

[5] *by E. Nesbit.*

the three posh London kids[6] whose father is sent to prison, and at the end all the real adults cry.

Well, they cried at our house anyway, specially when Daddy comes back and Bobby sees him on the station through the smoke and runs into his arms shouting, 'Daddy! My Daddy!'

Grandma passed the tissues.

Grandad said, 'Och another cold. It's so damp in England.'

And Dad just sat plopping fat tears onto Madge who was asleep on him.

I'd never seen him cry before.[7]

The 5th day, Dad went back to work wearing new squirty aftershave. I told him he smelt like wet upstairses on buses.

[6] *Bobby, Peter and Phyllis. And their mother takes them to Yorkshire to be poor in a cottage, only they're not as poor as us, because it's a big cottage and they have a field and a woman who cleans for them. It's all near a railway station and there's a porter called Perks and they have adventures like saving a train from a landslide and rescuing a boy who breaks his leg. And there's an Old Gentleman they wave to, and he helps them get their father back because they've been so nice all through the story.*

[7] *Why is it easier to cry at an old film that ends happily than it is to cry about . . . real things that won't end happily at all?*

He said, 'We like it, don't we Grandma?'

'It smells very clean and manly dear.'

'See!' my father said and went off to the building society – singing.

I finished the sherry trifle, and was sick.

On the 6th day, we children watched The Railway Children again.

Eliza said she was Bobby. Madge was Phyl who had to have her hair brushed a hundred strokes. I was Peter and Perks. Grandma was Mrs Perks who has all the babies, Grandad the funny Russian, and the Old Gentleman.

Eliza said we didn't have a Mummy.

On the 7th day she told *our* daddy he was Daddy and he said couldn't he be someone else as well? He didn't want to just be in prison?

'Well,' Eliza thought, 'you can't be mummy.'

'No . . .' Dad shrugged. 'Well, what about that other man who works at the station – not Perks but the man you just see opening the gate in the blurry distance?'

We stared at him, wondering if he'd been drinking again.

He said if we didn't believe there was such a man we'd just have to look at the whole film again.

So we did. And there *was*.

'See!' he said, in tears.

At the 'Daddy my daddy' bit where *their* Daddy returns home in a cloud of smoke, Eliza and Madge leapt onto *their* Daddy on the brown sofa, making him cry even more. Grandma had hiccups and emergency sherry.

When the girls were in bed, Grandma and Grandad babysat us, and *our* Daddy went out smelling like a bus, to let in the New Year.[8]

On the 8th day, Grandma made Grandad take her to church even if he was still poorly from whisky.[9] And Eliza made Grandma take *her*, even if she was wearing a white nighty over her clothes being Bobby.[10]

On the 9th day of Christmas Eliza pulled the chicken wishbone and said, 'I wish a Old Gentleman and . . .'

'It might help,' my father said.

'Cos if I had a Old Gentleman I could have my mummy back. Who do *you* wish, daddy?'

I said, 'Grown ups don't wish.'

'Do,' my father said, 'but I'm not telling you or it won't work.'

'Don't then!' Eliza said.

[8] *But who with?*
[9] *He was.*
[10] *She was.*

He never did.[11]

United lost 0-3, and Grandad drove Grandma back up the low road to Scotland.[12]

On the 10th day Dad went back to work again, in old aftershave, Auntie Marion brought a tin of shortbread biscuits, and we made her watch (all) The Railway Children while we ate them (all).

On the 11th day I had to go back to school.

At break Debbie Henderson was alone in the classroom monitoring the gerbils[13] and sifting dry sand for them.

She said, 'What you get for Christmas anyway?'

I told her.

She told me what she'd got, and what Father Christmas had paid for everything.

[11] *So we still don't know whether he got what he wanted in the end, either.*

[12] *If I've not said so . . . I do love them. Funny things kept happening to us, this year, though. And when funny things happen, you do forget to say some things. But I think this is the last time Grandma and Grandad are in the story, so – thanks folks!*

[13] *Bernard and Fred. Or Bernardine and Fred, or Bernard and Frederika, as they turned out. But they're another story altogether.*

'Your mum's not come home, Julian?'

'Christmas isn't over yet.'

She backcombed Fred but he[14] squealed and wet the new sand.

'Watch The Railway Children?' I said.

'No.'

'We did. Six times now.' I started to tell her the story. She would have liked it because it had a vanishing dad in it, like she had.

But Natalie Thingy yaffled in from the yard, pretending to love animals. And saying, 'And anyway, Julian Chandler's dad is still going out with that blonde[15] woman in that car Debbie cos she was seen again last Friday, sitting and talking and – '

I knocked the sawdust tray on the floor. 'My father was at work last Friday actually.'

'Oh was he, actually?' she said. 'Well my mum says he was actually sitting with his blonde in the car with the engine turned off in Manor Close see. Actually!'

'You'll get locked up for telling lies.'

'I'll tell my mum you say she tells lies and she'll come and get you.'

[14] *S/he*.
[15] *At least it was the same one.*

94

'My mum'll get you.'

'You haven't got a mum . . . and what you blushing for if it's not true then?'

'Been bending and anyway it's you who should be blushing.'

'Why clever?'

'Because of what Jamie Learmouth's been saying.'

'What?'

I lied . . . 'He says things about you.'

'What things?'

'You know.'

She looked worried. '. . . Naughty things?'

'Course.'

'I'll ask him then. But one of you's going to be in such trouble.'

On the 12th day Eliza sang carols in her sleep, and I went in to tell her she would bring us bad luck. She cried and woke Madge so I went in to *her* and lay under her baby duvet with her, talking, like . . . someone-else used to.

'Goo gii ann!'[16]

'I'm not surprised she's *not* come. It's hard to travel at this time of year. And Christmas is no time for Women.'

[16] *Julian*.

I drank what was left of the milk in her spouty cup and went to sleep with her.

When I woke up it was dark, cold, wet and . . . next morning.

Christmas was over.

No surprises.

Part Four

13 She Never Wore A Blonde Wig

But then there *was* a surprise.

On the second Saturday of the New Year. One of those long Saturdays when nothing happens, and nothing feels as if it's *going* to happen, even on telly.

I was playing snooker, Eliza was under the table, Madge was in bed. And Dad was in the bath with the door open so he could shout at us if there was any shouting.

And there was.

It was just after half past four.

'Hello, anyone at home?'

I opened the front door and let in black January smells of old leaves and water and – lemon?

'Hello Julian?'

'Hello – Miss Day.'

But was it Miss Day?

She hadn't any books. And – she smelt of lemon.

'Am I early?' she said.

'I don't know.'

'I think it's about twenty-eight and a half

99

minutes to five. So *am* I early?'

'I don't know where you are going Miss Day or what time you're supposed to be there.'

'I'm going here.'

I got another whiff of lemons, like warm Fizzbags.[1]

'If you've come for my library books,' I lied, 'I thought my father had taken them back.'

'He daren't come since the spilt milk, still no use crying. Didn't see you at the match Julian.'

'No, I've been losing at snooker.'

'Who've you been playing?'

'Myself.'

'You must be good then. Give you a game?'

I took her coat. She had a red dress with a buckle, and *no purple cardigan*.

'Do you have a sister Miss Day?'

'No. I always wanted a brother.'

'Me too . . . But I want doesn't get.'

'That's the saddest thing I've ever heard.'

'It's what grown ups say to children when we don't say please, but even when we say please we don't get.'

'It's still the saddest thing I've ever heard.'

[1] *Our Miss Day never smelt like that. Perhaps she wasn't our Miss Day but a different Miss Day, from the library police? Her twin sister? Or just the real Miss Day in plain clothes disguise,* as her own sister?

I led her up the stairs.

'Eliza is playing Jesus under my snooker table.'

'Is *she* winning?' Miss Day enquired.

'She thinks it's still Christmas.'

'So it should be. We let it end too soon, just when we're getting used to it, and before there's anything else to look forward to, don't we?'

Dad shouted through a cloud of bubblebath we never used to be allowed. 'Who was at the door, Julian?'

'Miss Day!'

'What did she want?'

'I'll ask her!' I turned to her on the step below me, in a warm cloud of Fizzbag. 'Miss Day, what did you want?'

'I've come for the party.'

'She's come for the party!'

He shouted, 'What party?'

'I'll ask her.'

'This one,' she said handing me a pink envelope with baboon writing and an invitation with red kisses.[2]

'She's come to . . . Eliza's party!' I shouted.

There was a splash.

[2] *See page 83 if you don't get it.*

Miss Day said, 'United were four one up[3] when I left to come here.'

'My father's in the bath with no clothes on Miss Day.' I waved her into my bedroom.

Miss Day said, 'It's a good idea, saves wetting your clothes.'

Eliza poked out from the table. 'Hello Miss Day. This is my baby Jesus. Do you want a go?'

'Yes please.'

Miss Day had a long go, till my Dad came in, rubbing his face with a towel. 'Now then, what was all that stuff about Miss Day coming to a party and oh –'

He clutched his dressing gown, a bit late. 'I'm terribly sorry Miss Day, I didn't realize you were really . . .' He was blushing like the baboon. 'The kids spend so much of their time pretending –'

Miss Day said, 'I think this invitation is pretend too.'

Eliza said, 'It's *real*. I took it to you in the library with Auntie Marion?'

Miss Day nodded, 'And Mrs Beacon will be very jealous when I tell her it's the best pretend party I've been pretended to be invited to. But I should only have pretended to come, of course. Goodbye.'

[3] *'We might lose today Julian but you just wait till later in the season.'*

'You mustn't go,' Dad said.

'No!' Eliza said, and winked.[4]

I went downstairs to make the party with my Dad.

'Poor Miss Day.'

'Not poor, Dad. She actually goes to football matches and she's nice and – '

'I meant the "poor Miss Day" who really came to a party that was only pretend.'

'It's not pretend, now.'

We made a green thing that didn't work. We opened some unlabelled fish in a tin that might have been Chonk's, found half a bottle of red wine, cake candles, nice biscuits, some old red napkins and three mince pies, probably from last year. Dad nipped out to the shop for a frozen Black Forest Gateau and prawn cocktail crisps.

He led the way upstairs with the picnic but stopped and shushed me outside my door.

Eliza was saying, 'My daddy doesn't shout only when we are very very naughty.'

Miss Day said, muffled, 'I used to think I could be very very naughty.'

I said, 'You know she wants Miss Day to be our mother?'

He said, 'Shhh. You've already got a mother.'

[4] *I didn't even know she could.*

But he was blushing again as he banged the door open with the tray, stumbled and splattered red wine all over my room.

Eliza was under the snooker table. But she was alone.

'Where's Miss Day?'

'Narnia,' Miss Day answered from inside my wardrobe.

My father came back with a towel to mop up. I noticed he smelt of fresh aftershave.

And Madge woke up.

We had the real pretend party downstairs while my room dried out. I secretly warned Miss Day not to have the pilchards because they might not be. Miss Day thanked me, and Madge cuddled her all party. Eliza wore her Bobby costume. I drank a glass of red wine, blushed and felt not really there.

We played musical bumps, dead fishes, in-and-out-the-dusky-bluebells, stomach pumps and libraries. Dad did some AMAZING(-ish) coin tricks.

'At six o'clock,' Miss Day said at six o'clock, 'their mummies and daddies will take them home to bed because they're tired little teddy bears.'

'I know that one,' Eliza said.

'I do, too. But I don't know what a "disguise" is,

do you? I think it might be a coat. And I must find mine.'

She gave us each an envelope with a £2 book token. My father said she shouldn't. She said what was wrong with books.

At the door, I asked if she ever went out in her car on Fridays.

'I don't think so. I haven't got a car.'

I was just about to ask her if she ever wore a blonde wig but Eliza sniffed, and said, 'You smell nicer this afternoon, Miss Day.'

We sometimes met Miss Day on purpose after that, in the park or outside the Crown on Sunday dinnertimes. She often smelt nicer but she never wore a blonde wig, or had a car.

14   We Still Need That Body

The last week in January our new school community policeman PC Hacker, came to school in all his uniform.[1]

Debbie Henderson arrested me and took me to him in the playground.

'Can Julian ask you something, PC Hacker?' she said.

'What I'm here for, dear.'

She looked at me.

I shrugged.

She said, 'Suppose someone vanished, PC Hacker?'

'I'm supposing.'

'What do the police do?'

'Depends on who's the someone who's vanished, dear.'

'Someone's relation?'

'We're all someone's relation, dear.'

'Say it was Julian's relation?'

[1] *except his truncheon.*

'I think Julian's relation would go on the missing person's file.'

'Then what?'

'Not much, dear. Most people who miss want to stay missing.'

She looked at me.

I shrugged.

She said, 'Suppose someone instead of vanishing had been murdered?'

PC Hacker tapped his helmet. 'If you're murdered you tend to leave a body.'

Debbie said, 'What if you've vanished first? And then been murdered after?'

'Mmm.' PC Hacker looked puzzled. 'We still need that body. They do turn up from time to time. Buried in shallow graves, dogs dig 'em up. Drowned in lakes, they float to the surface. Melted in acid baths, their teeth don't. You'll find most folk who vanish find it far too much trouble to be murdered as well dear.'

Debbie looked at me.

I shrugged.

She said, 'But suppose someone's mother vanished and never wrote or rang up? And say the next door neighbour got an idea she might have been murdered? And say that –'

'Still need that body dear and – here, you stop!' He waddled off across the playground, to chase three Infant Ones who were playing with the radio in his unlocked car.

She said, 'You didn't say much.'

'He shouldn't call you dear.'

'He was useless. But I've got a plan.'

15 The Cat'll Be Killed

But there was another plan first.

Three nights after PC Hacker, in the dramatic final
seconds of my surprise victory over Argentina
(11-1), my father invaded the pitch, and told me it.

It was:
1   to leave Number 77 (our home for ever) and
2   to move to Number 6 (a shop on German
     Street 8 miles away, in the middle of town).

'Shop?' I said, bungling the throw-in and feeling
sick as a woodpecker.
    'The owner's a Mr Dawson,' he said, 'and he's
keen on a quick sell because he's off to Australia.'
    'Pass the floodlights?'
    'And there's a Mr and Mrs Western who looked
round this house today and they're keen to buy.'
    'Linesman?'
    'I'll give up the building society and run the
sho–'

'Pitch?'

' – and I'll be able to look after you properly. Like when you were ill. It'll all b– '

'Can I have the pitch or not?'

The following Tuesday morning he had a letter.

'We're off! We're moving!'

'Bye bye then Chonk,' I said scratching her forehead just where it made her purr. 'Cats that get transferred keep going back home till they're run over. Splat, squodge, dead.'

'It's right opposite a swimming pool. And it's a *video* shop so you'll be able to watch them all free. And – '

'You'll be able to watch them all free,' Debbie Henderson said when I told her in the dinner queue.

'So?'

'But you'll have to go to a new school.'

'So?'

'Good thing,' she said. 'Cos Jamie Learmouth's after you for what you said about what he said about Natalie.'

'So?'

'He's a better fighter than you.'

'What's this plan you had then? About my mother?'

'Doesn't matter now, does it?'

Mrs Embleton called out round her chained front door. 'They tell me *you're* going away now?'

'It's my father's daft idea Mrs Embleton.'

'I get used to people. And then they leave me.' She was crying.

'If Chonk comes back looking for us, you can look after *her* Mrs Embleton.'

'I'm not bothered, you know. Not bothered.' But she sounded very bothered.

'We'll send you cards Mrs Embl–' I called. But she was locking her door and bolting it, and turning off her light.

I didn't talk to my father for five days, like my mother usedn't.[1] He sang, when he realized, like he used to with her. It never worked.

On the sixth day, Sunday, when he was shaving and singing, I cracked, 'And what school *shall* I have to go to, then?'

'We'll be on the 75 route, so you can stay where you are. But anyway by next week I might be able to –'

'You're not able to do anything,' I said, 'you just mess things up.'

'My fault is it?'

[1] *I kept thinking she'd still come back, just in time, and stop it all. Perhaps send* him *off round the world.*

'Course.'

'How?'

In a very quiet voice I told him how. '1) you made my mother vanish which you might think is an AMAZING conjuring trick. 2) – '

He didn't interrupt, or walk away, or tell me to shut or grow up, or any of that. He shaved and dabbed. Sometimes he nodded. My words just came. I got stronger, telling him how useless he was and how unhappy he'd made us all and –

I didn't start crying till nearly the end.

'Course,' I said, 'we're only kids and you can do anything to kids. Tell us lies. Do things behind our backs. Sing! But she was our mother and she's gone. And we've got to move into rotten town to a rotten shop, and the cat'll be killed and we'll have no friends – '

And the waterworks really started then.

'You'll have all your old friends and – ' he said, in the very low voice he used to try to calm her.[2]

'I didn't even get invited to Eric *Rickaby*'s party! And anyway no one'll be able to ring me up even if they want to because they won't know my number and – '

'We'll take our own number if that's what you want?'

[2] *That never worked either.*

112

'*I want doesn't get?* Don't you even know *that*?'

'Listen –'

'Never listening to you ever again. You're dead!'

16   Under New Management

I woke, early, and lay listening to the last morning
ever . . . the early Manchester train . . . Mrs
Embleton banging the teapot lid to show she'd
lived another night . . . Chonk at the kitchen
window like Peter Pan . . . Madge, Eliza and him
snorting and puffing in their own rooms for the
last time.

I put my mother's school photograph into the big
tobacco tin with holes in the side and the lid with
hinges Mr Embleton gave me for caterpillars when
things were all right.
   I buried it at the end of the garden with the dead
things.

At quarter to eight, before the girls were really up,
the removal men unloaded themselves. They had
teeshirts and tattoos, and they smoked cigarettes
and shouted.
   'Nice weather for flitting?'
   'Watch your back sunshine.'

They lifted us out of their way, swore as they trapped themselves on the stairs, called my father 'squire' and demanded noise.

'Got a radio, squire? Music while we work? If you call it work, eh, smashing up other folks' homes? Whoops.'

A man with tattoos even in his hair dragged a huge radio into the hall, and turned it on as loud as possible. The noise got bigger as the house emptied, and the men had to get even louder to hear themselves shouting and swearing.

My mother would never have allowed it.[1]

'What's your name little girl?'

'Not a little girl,' Eliza said.

'What's your name?'

'Haven't got a name.' And then, when the man went she called, 'And we haven't got a mummy!'

I took Eliza and Madge to the top of the house. All that was left was the smell of the men.

'Say bye bye to Mummy and Daddy's room.'

'Bye bye,' Eliza said.

'We'll never sneak up here again on Sunday morning and squeeze between them in bed.'

'No bed.'

[1] *But of course it was my mother who* was *allowing it. She was why it was happening.*

'No anything.'

I took her into every room, to remember and be sad in. You have to let your feelings out, like at a funeral, or you get ill with them staying inside you.

I let mine out.

'Bye bye red and white stripey cupboard she painted me that'll be here for ever for other kids to use . . . Bye bye toilet where we weed for ever but won't ever again.'

But we did, just once more, to say bye bye.

There was a trunk of my mother's things waiting for a different lorry to come and take them to Grandma's. Eliza found a green silk scarf in it, to sniff, and rub between her thumb and big finger, like she used to with her old sucky blanket. Madge went to sleep.

Some time by the middle of the afternoon Number 77 wasn't ours.

The front door had to be open for the removal men. I huddled with Eliza and Chonk in the bare front room. I told them about Debbie Henderson and her naughty sister, and anything else I could think of about anything that was nothing to do with our family.

Then Auntie Marion came in with Madge. 'Your Dad's gone over to Number 6 with the removal men. So we're off to a nice filling tea at my house.'

I said, 'No use crying Auntie Marion.'

'It's the dust,' she said and hugged Eliza.

'We're all crying Auntie Marion, cos we're leaving our mummy here,' Eliza said.

I said, 'We're saying goodbye to you too aren't we Auntie Marion?' I said. 'My father doesn't need you now either.'

'Shhhhh.'

I squodged Chonk into her new cat basket. The removal men's radio was yelling a song about people who loved people who don't love them.[2]

'Say bye, Number 77,' I said.

Auntie Marion squodged me.

'Let go! I want to wave bye bye to Mrs Embleton.'

I did, and I did.

But all her curtains were shut.

It was a nice filling tea.[3]

[2] *As if that's worth making a song about.*

[3] *e.g.: three different fizzy drinks; chocolate fudge cake and tip top cream; Worcester sauce crisps; jam and sugar sandwiches made of white bread with crusts cut off; as much tomato sauce as we wanted, whatever we wanted it with; a saucer of Smarties each; a garlic sausage; a red jelly shaped like a jelly and a green jelly shaped like a tortoise (but not much like one); a poached egg on buttered toast, called 'chicken in a raft' by Auntie Marion's Kevin; lots more.*

Auntie Marion said, 'It'll only be scratchings when you get home tonight.'

'Not going home tonight.'

'You *are*, chuck.'

Eliza said, 'Please may you come and live with us and be our mummy, Auntie?'

'And what would my Kevin do then, poor thing? Come on, eat up or it'll be dark, and then where will you be?'

'Lost,' I said.

German Street was very narrow. One side was just the brick Baths. The other side was Numbers 2 to 16, all joined together bricks. Everything opened straight onto the street. Instead of gardens, grass and trees there were chips, cars, curry and chlorine.

Number 6, ours, was the third shop down the left, next-door-but-one to the Taj Mahal Restaurant with a buzzing street lamp outside. We had two peeling blue doors, and peeling posters of films I'd never heard of all over the glass. There were two gold red and yellow notices saying UNDER NEW MANAGEMENT.

I took Eliza hand-in-hand up some steep stairs. A single bulb dangled.

'Say hello to your Number 6, Eliza.'

'Hello.'

'Horrible isn't it?'

'Yes.'
'Do you wish mummy was here?'
'No.'

I'd expected it to be as bare as 77 but of course it was crammed out with our stuff in boxes and tea-chests lined up to block the gloomy corridor that ran down the middle of the flat.

And . . . Miss Day[4] was putting up bookshelves in the kitchen.

My father said, 'Welcome home, Julian.'

I said, 'Which's my room?'

'Want to go down and have a look at the video shop first?'

'My room!'

It was the tiny one with a window over the street, close enough to touch the street lamp.

I wedged the door and let Chonk out of her basket. She did not leap at the window to kamikaze back home. I would have. I lay on the bed and she shivered onto me to stroke her till we both felt better.[5]

[4] ??????????????????
[5] *Stroking animals is good for you. Mr Hills told us about some old people in hospitals who borrow dogs on the NHS.*

Ages later my father poked round the door with a glass of beer.

'What do you think of Number 6, Julian?'

'It smells.'

'Other people's homes always do. Handy for swimming though?'

'You can't swim.'

'Want some froth?'

'No,' I lied. 'And you do know Auntie Marion's still outside with Madge?'

'Auntie Marion went ages ago. Madge and Eliza were zonked out and they're asleep in bed.'

'Is Miss Day in bed too?'

'Probably.'

'Which room?'

'. . . She's not here if that's what you think?'

'I don't think.'

I ignored him till he went. Then I went properly to bed in odd bits of pajamas and socks.

I had no curtains, and the orange light shone straight on me and Chonk. Some lads and a noisy girl stood shouting under it about why United had lost[6] again, till the pub closed and I couldn't hear them any more because of the cars and drinkers.

[6] 0-5.

16   Bust!

The following Monday morning, I saw something important, from the bus stop on London Road.
I didn't say anything.

When I came back I had a closer look.
I didn't say anything then, either.

Number 6[1] looked even tattier in daylight. It had been a grocer's years ago. There was always a smell of old cheese and coffee from the shelves, specially when it rained.
It always rained.

'Had a good day at school?'
'No.'
He was sitting on his shop counter in his suit and shirt. But he hadn't got a tie on, or any aftershave.
Eliza and Madge were piling up blank video

[1] *HYAVIDEO!*

cases, playing babies and the mummies that go with them.

There were no customers.

I said, 'No customers?'

'A lady in a hat came in for a video of a royal wedding only it turned out she thought you just put it in your telly. We haven't got a video of a royal wedding anyway. Nine customers brought films back.'

'Nobody came to take any out, course?'

'No – but why "course"?'

I scrambled eggs for everybody. We ate them down in the shop, because it didn't shut till nine. Two tiny kids came in from the Baths and asked if they could try out their Samurai fighting computer cassette.

I watched an old cowboy video and went to bed at midnight.

When I got home on Tuesday my father was playing mother-and-toddlers all round the shop, using video boxes. There were two other kids, as well as my sisters and Chonk. Eliza was bathing her babies.

'These are Satinder and Ali,' she said.

'No customers?'

My father said, 'I expect folk mainly borrow videos at the weekend.'

'When do they bring them back then?'

He shrugged. 'The longer they keep them out the more I get in rent. Hup Satinder!' And he caught her in mid-air, and turned her over and over till she chuckled till she was sick.

I went upstairs with an American disco dancing film but me and Chonk got bored with it, and played cats instead.

When I got back on Wednesday, there were nine kids sitting in a row in the shop window.

Eliza was being mummy to them and all the teddies, animals, dolls and Things that were lined up. Madge sat changing Chonk's nappy.

My father was in jeans and teeshirt, and the stained suede shoes with no heels he was supposed to have taken to Oxfam years ago. 'Hi Julian, want a ride on our family railcard?'

'No.'

'Had a good day at school?'

'No.'

'These are Rabinder and Shashi who live with Satinder and Ali at the Taj, then there's Mark, Matthew and Luke who live with the sweets and newspapers on the corner. And Nancy who must live somewhere but she can't remember, can you Nancy?'

'Ogggagagagagagag.'

Eliza said, 'Nancy is Madge's friend. The others

123

are all my friends. You haven't got any friends have you Julian?'

I was half way up the stairs as Eliza said, 'Please daddy may you show Julian the puppies show cos he hasn't any friends.'

'Ladles and jellyspoons, of course!' My father clapped. 'Shake your feets, the snow is a boat to come in!'

'I'll be their mummy, and make sure they are good,' Eliza said. 'Come on children! I'm mummy. I'll look after you.'

And the kids did just as she said, marching in pairs of dolls and animals round the shop and then up a ramp onto the counter. Singing.[2] Then they sat down in front of the counter and stared up.

'Goat laughter moons, ladles and jellyspoons!' my father shouted, and the show began.

It turned out to be only a *puppet* show,[3] with my father waggling the animals and dolls over the back of the counter telling a story in different voices about a zoo that the animals took over. Eliza kept nodding at her children to make sure they were good.

[2] *Who built the ark?*
    Noah Noah
    Who built the ark?
    Brother Noah built the ark.
[3] *I want doesn't get, see.*

They were, squelching and staring, thumbs in mouths. Even Chonk sat still, and wouldn't come to me for comfort even when I opened a tin.

It was obviously time for me to get a stick and red spotty hanky and go off down London Road to seek my fortune, like my own mother had done.

I went upstairs and scrambled the last egg.

'Something worrying you Julian?'

'Something worrying you Father?'

'No.'

'Is Mr Dawson in Australia yet?'

'I don't know. Why?'

'Nothing. Much.'

Chonk slept with Eliza and wouldn't come out even when I dangled frozen cod on a string over her.

On the Thursday I got back to find even more kids. This time they were outside, standing in a long queue in German Street, with towels.

He said, 'Have you got your key? We went for a swim and got locked out.'

Eliza said. 'I'm our mummy making sure we are good, aren't I daddy.'

I said, to him, 'You can't swim.'

'They're teaching me.'

'Who? Satinder, Rabinder, Shashi, Ali, Matthew,

Mark and – '

'The baths attendant is swapping me free lessons for free videos. I've been in the deep end. With arm bands, of course.'

'Bet you you looked daft.'

'Bet I did.'

'Any customers here?'

'Not today. I expect Friday's the big day.'

On Friday when I got back there were even more kids, and another cat. They were all sitting absolutely silent, watching my father AMAZE them with my Complete Boys stuff, while Eliza nodded to keep them good.

Nobody turned round to ask if I'd had a good day at school.

'Any customers?'

'One – returning three Kung Fu videos for someone who'd died. I couldn't really charge extra.'

'Still hoping for a weekend rush?'

'Got to be.'

'Won't be. Come and look at this.'

I led my ruined family up German Street, and out into the London Road.

'Look!' I said pointing at my secret, next to the greengrocers where I'd bought the eggs.

'Oh dear,' my father said, giggled and swore. And swore again. And giggled.

Madge brrrrmed on his shoulders.

Eliza said she wanted a banana.

For (my secret) – next to the greengrocers, was a double shop with flashing coloured lights right round the windows. Inside there were mirrors and arcade machines and a huge screen and millions of videos. There were posters in frames from every film you've ever wanted to see. And an electronic message saying –

'Opening bargains three for the price of two. Open seven till midnight. Free coffee and biscuits.'

There were five assistants in a red stripy uniform, all of them prettier than my father. And there were also all our customers, of course.

I said, 'What next father?'

He said, 'Shall we go home and look at our video of The Railway Children?'

'It's not home,' I said.

But we went there anyway.

About ten o'clock when my father had cried, I put the girls to bed, while he fetched fish and chips and beer.

'Well Julian,' he began, 'we're ruined. Bankrupt. Bust. Finished. Scrapheaped.' He paused. I said nothing. 'Done for. Kiboshed. KO-ed. Wrecked. Sunk.'

He shook his head, poured me some froth, and sipped.

I said, 'You'll just have to get out your shiny trousers again and go back to the building society.'

He shook his head. 'Can't. They paid me to stay away for ever.'

'We'll have to buy back Number 77, then.'

He shook his head. 'Can't. I used the money from selling Number 77, and the redundancy money the building society gave me, and what I borrowed from Grandma and Grandad, to buy this business.'

'There isn't any business.'

'No.'

'Didn't Mr Dawson tell you there was the brand new wonderful video hire shop ten times as big as ours just opening round the corner?'

'No, he was in a hurry to get to Australia. Ow.' My father cut himself on the beer can. 'Your mother used to talk about us running a wholefood café. But she could cook . . . I certainly can't Do-It-Myself. I don't even know what "It" is . . . There's already a pub and a restaurant and a news shop and . . . What'll I do Julian?'

'You'll have to wait for her to come back.'

He shrugged, poured me more froth, and sipped.

I said, 'She's not coming back is she?'

He shrugged. And looked at the blood on his thumb, puzzled by that and everything else.

So I said, 'I've got an idea.'

'Have you?'

'Want to hear it?'

'Course.'

'It'll change everything?'

'Tell me then.'

I told him.

He shook his head.

He poured me some more froth and I went over
the idea again. It sounded even better. I think the
froth made me a bit drunk really, whatever 'drunk'
is.[4]

'No,' he said again. 'I can't.'

'It's the only thing you've ever been any
good at.'

I went over it again.

At midnight we did our teeth together, and kept
bumping into each other. He put his arm round my
shoulder, and squeezed. 'You've been great since
your mother went, Julian.'

'I know. But what about the puppet show and
the kids?'

'You're so like your mother.'

'I know.'

[4] *It's sort of going fuzzy as if you're not quite there, even
though you are, and feeling quite happy, even though
you aren't.*

But I didn't know. And I didn't know whether I wanted it to be true, now, anyway.[5]

'So what about my idea?' I said.

'All right . . . if I have to.'

'It's a promise?'

'Yes.'

I shut my bedroom door and lay down just in time for the room to start spinning and the bed to float up and tip me out.[6]

[5] *And wants don't get, anyway, so you've more chance if you don't.*

[6] *That's what drunk is.*

17 My Daddy Did Not Go to Prison

To cut the long story short.

My father closed HYAVIDEO and reopened it as
The Magic Shop.

We became friends with Uncle Frank, who had
been a real circus clown till he lost his nerve, but
now hid in a red double decker Joke Bus.

My daddy did not go to prison.[1]

[1] *But he did learn to swim a length, nearly.*

Part Five

18   The Magic Boy

I came to my turn in Mr Fever's Friday House of
Commons[1] just before Easter.

I'd prepared my first speech, about football, last
October. I'd written the KEY WORDS on a card,

[1] *The rules of Mr Fever's Friday House of Commons:*
  - *Stand up at the front, and*
  - *Talk.*
  - *If you stop talking you have to go on standing till
  your three minutes are up (e.g. Jamie Learmouth
  stopped talking about his family tree, when he got stuck
  after 1 minute 28 seconds, when he mixed up his cousins
  with his nephews).*
  - *Mr Fever is Mr Speaker in a lawyer's wig that smells
  of hedgehog, and he shouts 'Order!'*
  - *When he does you start, or*
  - *Stop.*

like Mr Fever said real speakers do.[2]

But then Mr Fever banned football speeches because he said that it was time young people today had some real interests to talk about instead of talking about what they were really interested in.

So in December I'd prepared a second speech, this time about dying.[3]

But in January little Alan Davies did his grumbling appendix and his scar, and Jenny Holmes fainted. Then Georgie Donaldson did two minutes twelve seconds on her Nan-Nan's new teeth.[4] And Jenny Holmes fainted again.

On the Friday after, Norm Wilson did his speech

[2]*UNITED*
   MAKE BALL DO WORK
   BE HUNGRY FOR GOALS
   WHAT FOOTBALL ALL ABOUT
   SEASON NOT OVER YET
   SPORT FOR ALL
[3] *FLU*
   DREAMING OF DYING
   LAST WORDS
   OUT OF BODY EXPERIENCES
   BEREAVEMENT
   MAKING A WILL
[4] *They were in the kitchen drawer. Georgina sneaked in in the dark looking for mints. She grabbed for something white and they bit her and she had to be injected for lockjaw.*

on how he'd scalded himself with lentil soup because his family's gone green. And Eric Rickaby did one minute thirty-nine seconds on how he'd run under a tree in the park and scalped himself and the fire brigade had taken him to hospital for twenty-three stitches to hold his head on, only you can't see them because of his hair, so he brought some blood on a piece of cotton wool to prove it.

So Jenny Holmes was already very white when Natalie Thingy started on her mum's varicose veins being tugged out by the surgeon through a hole in her groin. Jenny Holmes fainted after twenty seconds. Mr Fever tried to catch her, and they were both off school for a week.

After that Mr Fever banned all blood, operations and death, as well as football. And Jenny Holmes was allowed to put up her hand whenever she wanted a speech to stop.

Uncle Frank gave me some advice from the days when he still had his nerve for performing.[5] And I prepared my third speech.[6]

[5] *But that's another story.*
[6] *ITCH*
   AMAZE
   GRAB
   STORIES
   FALSE END
   SELL
   SPEED UP etc.

And finally, just before Easter, gave it.

ITCH
I started by showing them a packet of itching powder. I dusted some on the inside of my wrist as I talked, and starting scratching without noticing as I explained the history of the itch.

AMAZE
Then I explained that a real magician did not even need itching powder – he (I believe in equal opportunities for women conjurors, but I've never met one[7]) can make a whole room itch with nothing. And when they didn't believe me I pointed out that they were all already scratching away.

This AMAZED them.

GRAB
Now I had grabbed their attention, I explained the secret of all live entertainment from lion tamers to vicars – grab the attention and keep it with regular new ideas.

STORIES
I told them the story of how my dad and I had started the joke shop. I told them the story of Uncle

[7] *Though I knew an AMAZING woman who'd vanished.*

Frank's red joke bus, and who he was and who he
had been before he had lost his nerve. I told them
what had happened the day he did.[8]

                    FALSE END
I pretended to stop. Then started to
                      SELL
  'I have one or two totally free price lists here for
the lucky few of you. On it are all the tricks, jokes,
puzzles, costumes, seven varieties of itching
powder, three varieties of ink blots, also stick-on or
paint-on boils, carbuncles, dog muck, dead fish,
chewing gum that turns teeth black – '
                    SPEED UP
  '– pimples, plasters with and without blood,
bloody eye patcheswaxyearsfalsenosesbroken-
noses, fingerswithandwithoutdirtyorbloodynails,
fake wounds, fatal wounds – '
                      ETC.
  Jenny Holmes's hand slid up.
  '– and nice trickstoo, kindtrickswithnopainin-
thematall – boy scout and cub tricks, and . . . stink-
bombsinthreesizes, draculateethwithjarofblood
andteeth marks, fourkindsofblacksoap, worms,
spiders, frogs and snakes – card tricks, burping
powders and pills, ventril–ventr– voice-throwing
aids, whoopy cushions, hairy palms, axestocut

[8] *Another story*.

                      139

yourownheadoff, knivestoamputateears and – '
  'Order!' Mr Fever ordered.

JOKE

'Thank you.' I ended on something funny, 'You *can* order from me in the cloakroom at playtimes and straight after sch– '

SIT

  'Sit!'
I sat. And the clapping started.
I had turned myself into – *The Magic Boy*.

19 Like Grandma On Sherry Trifle

I was being The Magic Boy and doing brisk
business with a kid from Mrs Hanns's in the
cloakroom after school on the Wednesday-but-one-
after, when Natalie Thingy yaffled in, followed by
Debbie Henderson who gazelled round the coat
hooks and stared without blinking.[1]

'Decided on your requirement yet sonny?'

'A plaster with real blood please Julian and a
phial of that stuff that makes feet smell and it adds
up to a pound.'

'Thank you sonny pleasure to do business with
you delivery at break tomorrow morning have a
nice day next please?'

Natalie Thingy said, 'Me.'

Debbie was still staring.

I wobbled like a Grandma on sherry trifle.

I loved Debbie Henderson!!! . . .

But I'd lost her by being careless . . . so careless I

[1] *Stare at the very end of the person's nose and think
about something very boring, e.g. Jamie Learmouth.*

could not even remember how I'd been careless.

My heart jigsawed.[2]

But I said, clearly, 'Yes girls, and what can we do you for?'

'We've seen rings in the window in your shop,' Natalie yaffled. 'So you needn't start telling more of your lies, you're in enough trouble, you wait till Jamie Learmouth gets you.'

Then Debbie spoke and her voice was softer than the silent snow in those see-through sort of eggs with a little cottage inside that you shake up and make silent blizzards in.[3]

'They were gold rings Julian and they were in a little basket.'

'Engagement rings, right? Someone is getting engaged to someone,' Natalie yaffled. She tapped my head. 'Anyone in?'

'Who's getting engaged?' I said.

'That's for someone to know and for someone else to guess and you'd better bring that ring to school tomorrow or someone'll get you.''

[2] *As in jigsaws that come in a thousand pieces and jigsaws that cut things up very brutally.*

    (You try writing your feelings down then, specially if you're a Man.)

[3] *I can get them for you for £1.50 each.*

'You better had Julian,' Debbie said, soft as black snow.

I looked for rings when I got back to the shop, and there weren't any.

I put it off till bedtime, then went down in my pajamas to find my Dad playing with a magic wallet at the counter.

'Watch very carefully.' He opened the wallet and there was a five pound note strapped into it. He shut it, and when he opened it, there was an Ace of Spades.

'Great . . . Dad?'

'See this?' He held up a toffee apple, and stuck out his tongue.

'Great,' I said. 'Dad there's some daft girl at our school says we'd got a basket of daft engagement rings in the window only –'

'We have. Tshshshsting!' He magicked a basketful from under the counter. 'By the way do you know how to make a Maltese cross?'

'Stamp on his foot. Can I have a ring?'

'Who for?'

'Some daft girl.'

'Why are you blushing?'

'You blush.'

'I know.' He gave me a ring.

I said, 'It's your fault I *do* blush.'

'Diddums.' He swooped over the counter,

grabbed my shoulders, and kissed my hair.

'Give over will you, Dad.'

'Nothing wrong with a bit of a cuddle.' He licked the toffee apple.

'You should have cuddled my mother a bit more then.'

'Praps. Here?'

'What?'

He pointed to his tongue. It had gone purple and smelt of aniseed. Or linseed. Or something else seedy and horrible.

'Ugh.'

'You can try it on Mr Fever, Julian? Get him to confiscate it and he'll not be able to resist a lick in the privacy of his study and then . . .'

It was a brilliant idea.

But I was getting a brillianter one.

20 Did I Say 78 per cent?

Two, by next morning.

1
I gave Debbie the engagement ring after
assembly.
'Ta.'
'And this.'
'What?'

2
'A toffee apple for Natalie Thingy.'
'Do you like her?'
'She's all right.'
'. . . Is that what you call her?'
'What?'
'"Thingy"?'
'Course.'
Debbie giggled and kicked me.

Anyway, that dinner time I was on the Infant steps
selling one of Mrs Hanns's kids a Japanese paper
goldfish you can eat, when Debbie came over with

Thingy. Debbie was limping for some reason.[1]

Natalie yaffled, 'Where's the ring then, July-Anne?'

I said nothing.

Debbie purred. 'He gave it me this morning.'

'Let's see.'

'I've put it somewhere.'

I thought Debbie was being very brave. Everyone knows what Natalie can be like.[2]

'Give my ring to *her* did you?' Natalie poked me.

'Yes.'

'Right then! We all know what's going on now Deborah Henderson. You were reckoned to be my best friend you. But you're my best enemy now. Shift.' She elbowed me where it hurts. 'You've had it now, you two.'

And she yaffled off.

I got up off the floor. 'It's only fair boys aren't allowed to hit girls in this school isn't it?'

Debbie said, 'What you staring for?'

'Where *did* you put the ring?'

'Want it back now do you?'

'Course not.'

And she limped off, the other way from Natalie Thingy.

[1] *See page 151.*
[2] *She was getting like it now.*

I waited for customers as usual at the end of school. Kids came in to make kissing noises on the back of their hands and sing the wedding march, and say what Natalie was spreading. I heard one of Mrs Freestones's say, '– and she'll have to be changed on the register to Debbie *Chandler* and she'll have to kiss Julian Chandler even when she doesn't want.'

I had no customers.

My two brilliant ideas hadn't been very.

So I had another.

3

I went back into Mr Hills's. He was frowning at his register.

'Your um Dad'll be expecting you Julian?'

'Big boy now, Mr Hills.'

'He seems to be coping better on his own these um days, but I must . . . 78 per cent of 363?'

'He's not on his own any more. He's got a blonde girl friend actually.'

'Um?'

'On Fridays.'

'Um.'

'But I'm in bad trouble Mr Hills and I've got a brilliant idea if you'll help me, please?'

'Um. Did I say 78 per cent?'

'Yes, but my idea – '

And I told him some of the bad trouble, and all of

the brilliant idea.

'Um brilliant,' he smiled. 'But where did I get 78 per cent from?'

Dad said I was brilliant too, and gave me thirty-one gold rings and a false ear.

Next morning after register Mr Hills made a speech about the generosity of The Magic Boy and The Magic Shop. And then gave everyone a gold ring.

He asked Dave Wasp to come out to the front and put his mucky fingers flat on the board for Georgie Donaldson to draw round. Then Mr Hills numbered the fingers and said what each means with rings on, and we had to copy our own hands neatly and label them, and then we could put our own rings on whichever fingers we wanted.

We did.

Then he told the story of his grandmother who had only just got married when she dropped her strangely marked wedding ring down the sink. She didn't dare tell her husband, but she sent for the sewer men and they searched for days with candles among the big rats.[3]

Anyway at the Grandmother's wedding anniversary dinner fifty years later they ordered a large fish and Grandfather bit on something

[3] *Jenny Holmes waved.*

hard.[4] And it was the strangely marked gold ring. He gave it to Grandma who wore it again, and luckily he hadn't noticed she had not had it for fifty years.[5]

But she'd got fatter so she could only just squeeze it on, and it stayed there for ever even when she was buried. And in fact it's still glittering gold among the bleached bones and the chubby worms.

After Jenny Holmes came round, Mr Hills asked us for *our* stories about rings. Georgie Donaldson told about how her Nan-Nan's ring got so tight when she turned diabetic that her blood stopped in her finger and she had to have it cut off.

Jenny Holmes thought it was the *finger* that was cut off and fainted again.[6]

Then Jamie Learmouth tried to impress Natalie Thingy by telling the story of Bilbo Baggins the hobbit and an invisibility ring cos he'd seen the daft play of it somewhere. Nobody listened because he kept getting his dwarfs, goblins and elves mixed up.

After dinner we painted rings, for a display on

[4] *Jenny Holmes waved again.*
[5] *Men!*
[6] *So Georgie Donaldson couldn't actually tell us whether this was the same Nan-Nan whose teeth bit her in the kitchen drawer.*

rings, and did short but descriptive writing on rings, to display with the paintings of rings, if it was neat enough.

After afternoon break we did circumferences, so that when we bought rings for our fiancé(e)s they'd at least fit.

At the end of the afternoon Eric Rickaby gave his ring back to Mr Hills and said could he do proper work tomorrow please.

Debbie caught me in the corridor.

'I know why you gave us all those rings, Julian Chandler.'

'Why then?'

'Because you reckon that now everyone's got a ring nobody's going to be bothered about you giving me one yesterday.'

'Ow. What you kicking me for?'

Two cleaners were half way down the corridor with their woolly brushes and the sand that smells of sick because it gets put down in the Infants's, when they're sick.

So I had to be fast. 'You know me and this girl in Chester?'

'The one you made up?'

'I've dumped her.'

'On bonfire night your dad told me you never go to Chester.'

The brushes were three-quarters towards us now.

'Anyway,' I said, 'we *can* be engaged now, if you want.'

'*We* can? You and me can you mean?' She giggled. Yaffled, nearly.

'. . . If you didn't want to, what did you want a ring for?'

'It was Natalie wanted it.'

I blushed all over. Then mumbled, 'But you kept it?'

The cleaners stopped a brush away, smiling.

She said, 'If we *are* engaged you can walk me down the school gate.'

She held my hand. I could feel the gold ring on her engagement finger.

We didn't talk. You don't have to when you're engaged. Besides she was limping again.

At the gate she took off her ring, and put it in my palm.

'Don't you *want* it after all that?' I said.

'This is the one Mr Hills gave me. Yours is in me shoe.'

'And that's why you're limping of course.'[7]

'*You'll* have to limp from now on. But it's only a secret engagement.'

'Eh?'

'Our Gloria's always got rings in her shoes from secret fiancés.'

[7] *Of course!*

151

'Why've *we* got to be secret?'

'Because of what dads do to mums when they're engaged and married.'

'Eh?'

'My mum says when men get old they always fall for younger women and then they just dump the women who've looked after them till then.'

'That's not what my Dad's done.'

'I reckon he's done yours in, like Mrs Emblething said.' We reached the gate. 'Kiss me if you want, if we're engaged?'

I sort of stood.

She sort of giggled. 'You don't have to.'

And she ran to the corner, unstuck Natalie's toffee apple from her pocket, and started licking.

21　The Actual Scene Of The Crime

Her tongue was purple and still smelt seedy next morning, but she hadn't noticed, and I didn't say.

She said if I was secretly engaged, I had to be interested in her new plan for after school, and go with her on it, however scared I was.

I was, was, did, and was.[1]

'My foot hurts,' I said at the top of the woods. 'The ring in my shoe's cutting right into the ball of my foot.'

'You get used to it.'

'And my father doesn't know where I am.'

'My mum thinks I'm with you, solving a murder.'

I stopped on the railway bridge. 'The Manchester Express's due.'

'So?' she said.

'It always comes at this time.'

'What time?'

[1] *engaged, interested, go, scared*.

'Now.'

'Good – so now come on.'

I came on, slowly. I said I couldn't remember which our house was anyway.

'It says 77 on that gate,' she said.

'It doesn't.'

But it did. Everything else had changed too. No canary car on the wobbly tarmac. No wobbly tarmac, even. There were purple paving stones and tubs of tiny trees. There were curtains, neatly drawn. There were no posters for Africa, Women or peace. There was no –

'What's up now, Julian Chandler?'

'When I used to come home from school sometimes there'd be a party. Or a meeting. And the house would be full. But other times there'd be nobody in at all. Or she'd be in bed, or in the bath or up the garden. On my birthday, last July –'

'Is that why you're called July-Anne?'[2]

'– She jumped out from that wall and picked me up and carried me out to the canary car and never said anything, just drove me off to Bridlington. But the clutch pedal fell off at York and we had to stay in a big hotel there, and we didn't get any sleep because she said we had to

[2] *I'd never thought of it.*

154

get our money's worth in the sauna and jaccuzi all night and – '

'No need to roar about it.'

'It's the wind – and my foot.' I told her about the photograph in the tobacco tin buried with the dead pets under the bluebells.

She said, 'Finish off the Fizzbag if you want.'

I sucked sherbet up one of the liquorice straws while she blew down the other, till it went up both our noses and we snorted everywhere.

She said, 'Anyway, my dad never came back for me. And he's still alive and that's worse than you. At least your mother's murdered.'

'Daft. Ow.'

'I'm going to see who's in.'

She skipped across the road so I couldn't see if she was crying too.

I shouted, 'They're called Mr and Mrs Western if they're in!'

'What they called if they're not?'

She rang the door bell.

I shouted, 'It doesn't work!'

But it did.

I chewed the liquorice straw, counted lamp posts, and waggled my toes to try to shift the engagement ring in my sock.

Mrs Embleton upstairs waved. I didn't wave back in case she thought I was trying to look in her bedroom and sent for PC Hacker and he came

round and she let it out that she thought my
mother had been murdered, and my daddy ended
up in prison, like the Railway Children's.

'There's nobody in,' Debbie said, back at my
side. 'And what you looking in women's bedrooms
for?' She waved at Mrs Embleton. 'She was the one
who first said your mum was murdered isn't she?
What you gone red for?'

'My liquorice won't suck.'

'Suck mine. We'll die of the same mystery
disease and Mr Fever will do an assembly about
what happens if we aren't hygienic. And you'll
blush because everyone'll know we're lovers.'

Our old back yard was filled now with orange
flagstones, and white pots with plants, a seat and a
sundial. There was a new lawn and fence. At the
very top of the garden there was a chalet with a
balcony. The trees had all been lopped and the sun
was shining where it never had in all my life.

She was at the back door. 'Where did you used
to leave the key?'

'It never shut after my dad broke the lock.'

'It's shut now. That the attic up there?'

'Course.'

'Our Gloria says dead bodies are usually kept in
attics or cellars. Lift me on this and I'll pull you up
after me and you can push me in through that
w-aaaah!'

156

And *she* vanished, leaving me on my own as the back door unchained, unlocked and unbolted.

Ten minutes later we were both dangling from tall stools at the new Breakfast Bar where our old stove used to be, drinking cocoa with – Mr and Mrs Western.

There was a new electric cooker by the window, a microwave, and a rack of little labelled jars where the pinboard used to flap with newspaper cuttings, posters, red bills, meetings and poems.

'Right,' said Mr Western, 'so what *is* going on?'

There were no smells of burnt sausage, milk, coal, garlic or cat – no *us* at all. Everything now smelt of squeezy air fresheners my mother banned, because they make the whole house stink like Men's lavatories, and destroy the sky.

Mrs Western said, 'There's really nothing to cry about now Julian.'

'Got a cold coming Mrs Western,' I sniffed. 'And the Fizzbag got up my nose the wrong way.'

'And his foot hurts,' Debbie added, nibbling her third chocolate biscuit.

Mr Western bit on a pipe without any tobacco. 'I still don't understand why you were trying to climb onto my roof?'

I nearly said it *wasn't* his roof and –

'Well,' Debbie said, 'you know I told you I was looking for a football only I must have come to the wrong house?'

'Uh huh?' Mr Western said, chewing his pipe.

'Well I *wasn't* looking for a football and it isn't
the wrong house. I'm Julian's girl friend you see.
And we're secretly engaged aren't we?'

'Yes,' I said, blushing.

'He's only blushing because he's embarrassed.
It's not because he's lying.'

'Uh huh.'

'And anyway I came to the last birthday party
he had didn't I Julian?'

'Yes,' I lied.

'It was last July. That's why he's called Julian.
And I was wearing an engagement ring, wasn't I?'

'Yes,' I lied.

'My grandma's grandma gave it to me when she
knew she was going to die.'

Mr Western looked at his pipe. 'She must have
been very old?'

'Yes, that's how she knew she was going to die,
Mr Western. But my grandad's grandad had
bought her that ring years ago but it had been lost
down the sink for fifty years and then they found
it in a bag of fish and chips. So it was very
precious you see?'

'Uh huh.'

'Anyway at this party of Julian's we played kiss
catch, and Julian caught me, didn't you?'

'Yes,' I lied.

'He didn't catch Sandra Perry or Ali O'Shea or Dolly Wild or Natalie Thingy or any of them.'

'Of those,' Mrs Western said softly.

'No, Mrs Western.'

'"Thingy" is an odd surname,' Mr Western said, biting. 'Natalie Thingy, uh.'

'Yes Mr Western. But he still didn't catch her even though she kept stopping. But anyway I had the ring on my finger, and this is my engagement finger, isn't it Mrs Western?'

'It is, dear,' she said. She was twisting her own rings, and looking soppy.

'Well,' Debbie went on, 'I lost it while we were chasing. The engagement was off, of course. Then Julian moved house, as you know. But at school we've just been doing a project on rings, you can ask Mr Hills if you don't believe me, and Julian remembered something.'

'What dear?' Mrs Western whispered.

Debbie said, 'We'd forgotten to look in the attic. Or the cellar. But we'd gone there to kiss hadn't we Julian? . . . *I'm* blushing now . . .'

And she was!

Mrs Western smiled. 'There's nothing to be ashamed of in blushing just as there's nothing to be ashamed of in . . . love and kissing is there, Mr Western, dear?'

Mr Western bit his empty pipe, shrugged,[3] examined a spice jar, and said, 'I still wonder why you didn't just knock at the door?'

'I rang the bell that wasn't working when Julian lived here.'

'Corroborated,' Mr Western said.

Mrs Western said, 'Mr Western used to be an inspector in the police didn't you dear?'

'Oh,' Debbie said, 'I don't suppose he believes me then.'

'You learn to believe a great deal in the Force,' he said, biting. 'I suggest we now go and visit the scene of the crime?'[4]

Debbie said, in a little voice, 'May I use your toilet first Mrs Western?'

Mrs Western took her upstairs.

Inspector Western asked me what team I supported, and told me what football was all about[5] while he collected three large torches,

---

[3] *Men are no good with their emotions (but we know that by now).*

[4] *I nearly said, like they do at the end of police films, 'But my father didn't commit the crime of murdering my mother'.*

[5] ● *Being hungry for goals,*
   ● *Getting stuck in,*
   ● *Using the whole pitch,*
   ● *Letting the ball do the work.*

a ground plan of the house, a bunch of keys and a notebook.

Debbie came back, and held my hand. 'I've been thinking of all the horrible things that get left in attics and cellars – skeletons and that, on shelves or in cobwebby trunks, or water tanks, or under loose floorboards, in bits, covered by new carpets or behind new brickwork . . .' And then she said, in a very little voice, 'So do you mind if I don't come Mr Western?'

Mrs Western put her arm around her. 'We'll leave this one to the men, dear.'[6]

So Inspector Western showed just me round my own home. Everything smelt wrong of course – flowery soap and spray and clean carpets.

There was a new green Robin three-wheeler in the cellar, and a carpet. There were fitted shelves and central heating in the attic.

I couldn't find my mother's dead body anywhere.

[6] *It was as if my mother and her ideas and campaigns and fights and arguments had never lived here.*

But . . . I *could* find the missing ring.[7]

We had more cocoa. Mrs Embleton came round and said hadn't she seen me in the street just now looking in her bedroom? She said what nice neighbours the Westerns were because they had mended the fence, and she liked seeing a man with a pipe in the garden again. She did not ask about my mother. Debbie showed her the engagement ring. Mrs Embleton said she looked very young, but everyone did these days.

Then Inspector Western drove us home in his three-wheeler, at 20 miles an hour.

[7] ● *She took off her shoe in the toilet.*

● *She took out the ring from her shoe.*

● *She sneaked it into my hand when she came down from the toilet.*

● *I kept it hidden in my palm.*

● *I 'found' it in the cellar under the three-wheeler and showed it to Insp Western, who called off the hunt.*

● *I offered it back to her in the kitchen.*

● *Nobody believed a word of it.*

● *Nobody said they didn't.*

● *Mrs Western asked me to do it properly and romantically.*

● *I did.*

● *I blushed.*

Next morning Debbie was waiting at the bus stop.

'*Did* you find any dead body last night?'

'Course not.'

'Did you look under the floorboards and behind newly bricked-up walls?'

'Course not. Even my dad'd not be daft enough to sell his house to a policeman when he'd just done a murder in it.'

'It's just the clever kind of thing murderers do do.'

'He'd not be clever enough then.'

'Probably didn't murder her then?'

'Never thought he did.'

We limped through the school gate together.

'Anyway,' I said, '*you* weren't clever with all that stuff about your grandma's grandma's ring. She'd have been about 120 years old.'

'Our Gloria says if you're going to tell lies, tell whoppers. But I've got another plan.'

I asked how she made herself blush.

She said it was because she was clever.

I said she wasn't that clever.

She said why not?

I said had she looked at her tongue lately?

She tried, but she couldn't.

Part Six

22 The Mystery's Solved
    (In Thirteen Parts)

One   Her Next Plan

Her next plan turned out mainly to be her having a
swim at the German Street baths every Friday,
while I cooked her tea at Number 6.[1]

I cooked from books Miss Day sneaked to me
from the library[2] . . . I did Spanish omelettes,
chilli con carne, pasta with tomato and garlic,
moussaka, Chinese chicken wings with ginger,
savoury pancakes, baked Alaska, deep fry
pizza etc.

Debbie never helped cook of course, because her

[1] *I went round her house sometimes but there was never
    any tea and there was always next door's new baby
    yelling through the wall.*
[2] *Our family had finally been invalidated by Mrs Beacon,
    when another twenty-three books were found missing in
    March, and never found.*

plan, after her swim, was to poke round the flat, looking for clues about my invalidated family.

'Your sisters are more disturbed than you were, Julian.'

'How'd you know? And do you like that sweet and sour fish?'

'Yes. Because Eliza says can I be her next mother and Madge has just started biting.'

'They might have turned out like that anyway.'

I told her she could cook something if she wanted. She said she couldn't cook. I said she could read couldn't she. She said something rude. I said she should have a talk with Sandy.

And I bribed her round Sandy's, one Friday, for Sandy to point out how men and women are equal these days and both have to do their share. But Sandy only said Debbie was a very interesting person, and gave me a hard jigsaw of Tower Bridge to do in the hall while they talked with the kitchen door shut. And there were six pieces missing anyway.

Debbie went to Sandy's on her own sometimes, after that. But she didn't get any more equal, except that she said we couldn't be engaged any more because Sandy had explained how marriage was bad for Women.

My father started growing a beard.

Debbie told him it didn't make him particularly

macho because he was one of the New Men who were coming who would treat Women better, and anyway it did suit him, and made him look even cleverer and kinder.[3]

Two   On the Seventh Friday

On the seventh Friday, tea was a three-cheese-salad with French apple torte and fresh cream.

She burped and said, 'My mum's getting divorced.'

'Good . . . Isn't it?'

'She's only doing it so she can get married again.'

'Who to?'

'Whoever turns up. She says the divorce goes in the newspapers, and then you get invited on dates again . . . Course, it means my dad really is *never* ever coming home.'

'Still want him to?'

[3] *Than me.*
    I liked her mother actually, even if she did laugh at me for using long words and cooking for her daughter. There was one night when me and Debbie talked about swapping parents, or getting them to marry each other. But that was before we decided marriage was bad. Isn't it funny though, how your parents like other parents' kids better than their own? We ought to run a bring and buy sale.

'Course.'

'After five years?'

'. . . I can't remember him really. Only what his hands smell like . . . And him calling me – '

'What?'

'You dare laugh Julian Chandler?'

'Course not.'

'Rosebud.'

I laughed. She kicked.

Three   On the Ninth Friday

On the ninth Friday she was leaning out of my window being rude about the people below while I served up the cauliflower au gratin. The girls were at the Taj eating papadums and playing happy families with Rabinder and Co.

Everything felt as if everything was going to stay like this, for once.

It was a good feeling.

Then Debbie said, 'Wow!'

And then, 'Quick!'

And then, 'The mystery's solved Julian!'

She tugged me to the window.

'I'm trying to do the caulifl– '

'Look, daft!'

A white Metro two-door was jerking between the parked cars, down German Street.

My father was driving.

And there was a blonde in the passenger seat.

'Wow!' Debbie said. 'She *is* much younger than him. Just like Natalie's mum said.'

'My father can't drive!'

'Anyone can tell that,' Debbie said, as he squodged the gears of the Metro, roared, banged and died.

I said, 'I don't mean he can't drive I mean – he *can't* drive! He's never learned.'

'Stepmothers shouldn't be pretty.'

'He's *driving*!'

'Not. He's got out. She's shuffling over onto the driver's seat. He's bending at her window. They're – kissing!'

And they were. I'd never seen my dad kiss any other woman but my mother.[4]

'Bet that beard tickles,' Debbie giggled.

Cars hooted till the blonde drove the Metro off down German Street. My father walked backwards to our shop, punched his fist in the air, and stood laughing under the window.

'Wow!' Debbie said, and then, 'Ain't love wonderful! ' And then, 'I could gozz[5] onto his bald spot.' She giggled. 'Jamie Learmouth did that to *his* dad when I was round his bedroom. His dad

[4] *And then not often, even when she was on the squodge.*
[5] *expectorate.*

came up to us and Jamie reckoned it was a bird
done his business on him and – '

Four   What Were You Doing in Jamie Learmouth's
       Bedroom?

'And what were you doing in Jamie Learmouth's
bedroom?'
   'Nothing.' But she blushed.[6] 'He was . . . sort
of my sort of boy friend but only for a little bit. Till I
swapped with Natalie.'
   'Swapped what?'
   'You . . . Natalie loved *you*, then.'
   'She didn't.'
   'She wrote you a letter from "an admirer".'
   'And she spelt it wrong – but that was *you* . . .
wasn't it?'
   'Her.'
   'You and Jamie were – ?'
   'And you're jealous! Sandy says Men being
jealous – '
   'Not jealous!'
   'Where you going now then?'
   'I'm going to talk to my own father if you don't
mind? Your tea's there if it's not too much trouble
to eat – Rosebud.'
   I sauntered.

[6] *Her!*

172

She shouted, 'Jamie Learmouth wanted to swap back. And . . . he still does! And . . .!'

Five   I Dashed

I dashed down to the shop.

Uncle Frank was stitching up a gorilla costume that had just come back wounded from the Townswomen's Guild.

'Hi Julian,' he said. 'What's the difference between a well-known sea bird in a storm and a footballer with jelly in his boo–'

'Can't wait. Dad's outside – '

'Yes and I think he's got a surprise for you and – '

But there was no time for surprises and ands.

I was out in the street –

Dad was on the other side by a green A Reg Bedford van with sliding doors and no bonnet. He was wiggling keys . . . at the driver's door.

I called, 'Dad!' Then, 'Aaaaaaaghahagah!'

I crunched with terrible pain in the middle of my left side exactly where Deborah Henderson had just punched me. Far off she was saying, 'You never ever call me Rosebud again, you, Julian Chandler! And Jamie Learmouth is a better kisser than you anyway – '

I gasped over the road, just as my father unwiggled his door.

'Aaaagh.'

'What do you think, Julian? Ours? Very cheap on petrol. Should just be able to get the Punch and Judy in the back too. Magic eh?'

'Aagh.'

Deborah Henderson was alongside again. 'He's jealous Mr Chandler and he just saw you with your girl friend.'

'With my – ?'

'The blonde in the car.'

He slid the back door open. 'Get in, both of you.'

Six   You Can't Drive

'You can't drive.'

'What's this say then?' He fumbled in his trousers for a scruddy sheet of paper with green print.

'What does it say Mr Chandler?'

'It says Jonathan Chandler (Mr) passed his driving test. This afternoon!' He turned the key in the ignition, and the engine snorted and died. He said, 'I bought this van last week so I would *have* to pass my test this time. Get in, and we'll celebrate.'

He turned the key. The engine juddered. She got in.

I got in the back with her. The engine yelped but stayed started.

And then he started talking. 'Biting-point, handbrake, signal. No – mirror, signal manoeuvre, position speed and look, and here we go. Go! Out we come, oooh, and straighten up, into second, it's a bit narrow here, am I all right offside, check the wing mirror and keep the gas going, traffic lights in front, hazard, down a gear, second, clutch down, select first, seven seconds handbrake, but no need if we, yes off up into second and – '

He was good at talking. What he was no good at was driving.

He wasn't quite fast enough to hit the black taxi at the end of German Street because its driver swung right onto the pavement, almost into Matthew, Mark etc. who were swapping smelly–looking things outside the baths.

'Sorry.'

The van stalled three times up the little alley into High Street and then jerked out at the side of the Nippa that wasn't nipping fast enough.

'Sorry!'

His side mirror sliced off.

'Someone can have it as a souvenir,' he said.

A man on a bike banged all the way down our van, waved in the back mirror with one hand till he fell off.

'Sorry?' My father bent lower and zipped into the side street into the market, which is one way,[7] scraped back, and reversed too fast into High Street, causing major accidents back to Rotherham.

An hour later we finally gasped up into the car park of the Peacock Inn, seven miles out of town, where the sheep start.

Dad said, 'Good driving eh?'

'Yes, Mr Chandler,' Deborah Henderson said. But she was as white as Jenny Holmes.[8]

Seven   *He Bought Dandelion and Burdock*

He bought Dandelion and Burdock for himself, because he said he'd never drunk it since he was a child, and cokes and six bags of tomato sauce crisps for us.

Then he just stood grinning at the wet sheep.

Deborah Henderson yaffled, 'Mr Chandler?'

'Sorry, right,' he grinned. 'Business. Now Debbie says you saw me with my blonde girl friend?' He burst his crisps bag like kids do. 'Well, she's called Hilary.'

'She's very pretty,' Deborah Henderson said. 'I suppose she is.'

[7] *Not his.*

[8] *He hadn't frightened* me. *Nothing could, any more.*

'Is she nice as well?'

'I found her rather – strict.'

'Julian needs someone a bit strict Mr Chandler.'

'She runs a very strict *driving school*.'

Eight Our Crisps Crunched

Our crisps crunched. The wet sheep baaaa-ed. His beard misted.

'A driving school?' Deborah Henderson yaffled. 'So – the blonde? In the car? Sitting talking? On Friday afternoons? She was – '

'You think you're so clever, Deborah Henderson,' I said.

My father nodded. 'I was her worst pupil for twelve years. But . . .' He grinned at the sheep. 'Forty-six hours of lessons and four tests later and I *can* drive. Well, nearly.'

'You didn't tell Julian about your driving lessons, did you Mr Chandler?'

'I wanted it to be a surprise.'

'It wasn't,' I lied.

'Everyone kept telling me how useless I was you see.' He was grinning again. 'I didn't want to give them any more evidence of my uselessness.'

He put his hand out to me. I moved.

'But even if she is your driving teacher, Mr Chandler, you could still marry her?'

'No. She's married. And so am I. To Julian's mother.'

'Where *is* she then?'

'I don't *know*.'

'Really really?'

'Really really really.'

Sheep. Crisps. Beard.

'Some people think she's dead, Mr Chandler.'

'. . . Do they?'

'Yes, and some people even think she's been murdered . . . By you.'

He walked away to the sheep.

I called. 'Deborah Henderson tells lies. Like you!'

'I do, Mr Chandler!'

Nine *Deborah Henderson Whistled*

Deborah Henderson whistled. The Derbyshire rain shone in her black hair. She was beautiful. No wonder Jamie lov–

Nobody loved me. It didn't matter. Not bothered.

She said, 'Jamie Learmouth never kissed me. Not really.'

Ten *My Father Grinned*

My father grinned back from the sheep.

She sucked and said all quiet, 'Why didn't Mrs Chandler ever ring up, wherever she'd got to?

178

She'd left poor Julian and his sisters as well as you. She could have sent them a card, even if she thought you *were* useless, couldn't she? . . . Are you sure Mrs Chandler did *really* set off round the world at all?'

He shrugged. 'She said she was when she rang me up from the airport. But no doubt when the police come to arrest me they'll check if she was on any planes that night.'

'Why didn't you stop her going, Mr Chandler?'

'Nicky wasn't the stopping kind of person, was she Julian?'

'But if when she rang up Mr Chandler you'd told her you loved her and – ?'

He shook his head.

Eleven   Didn't You Love Her?

'*Didn't* you love her?' she said.

I breathed in.[9]

He spoke, nearly too quietly, with all the baaing and crunching. 'I loved her for a long time Debbie. We had three children together. She was the most amazing woman I've ever met. I wasn't a very amazing man.' He grinned.

'*Are!*' she mumbled, as if the next thing she was

[9] *Eliza and Madge believe it makes you invisible. It seems to work.*

going to do was squodge him.

'We've all changed a bit since last September haven't we Julian?'

He held out his hand. I didn't take it.

Twelve   There's Another Surprise

'There's another surprise I'd better get over,' he blushed. 'I don't suppose it will *be* a surprise though, because you kids are so quick these days. You were talking about my "girl friend". I feel a bit old for "girl" friends but – '

He shrugged.[10]

Deborah Henderson nodded help.

He went on. 'There's no question of . . . and anyway . . . besides I've got three wonderful kids and I live with them and love them and . . . Miss Day's my girl friend if I've got one at all. That's my last surprise Julian.'

'Knew anyway,' I sort of lied.

'I didn't!' Deborah Henderson said, giving him the squodge that had been waiting all afternoon. 'And don't you worry about us telling people Mr Chandler because we keep secrets don't we Julian? We're engaged as well you see and we've never not told no one never.'

[10] *Men do.*

'You just told him,' I said. 'And anyway we're *not* engaged.'

'Nor are Miss Day and me,' he said.

'Well *I* am,' she said.[11]

He said, 'I hope you'll be very happy.'

She said, 'I hope you will.'

We all stared at the misty sheep.

Thirteen   *I Want a Dog*

'I want a dog,' I said.

And he said, 'And if you want a dog Julian . . . you can *have* a dog.'

[11] *So you go and eat your woggle, Jamie Learmouth.*

23   I Want Gets

So, anyway, it's Thursday night now. Three weeks after the crisps and the sheep. I'm babysitting myself and the girls while Dad and Miss Day have an Indian meal at the Taj.

I've got the metal comb, a newspaper and the powder that makes you sneeze. I'm de-fleaing Chonk ready for my dog.

'I'll choose you one that's not too big, Chonk. I wondered about a King Charles sp–'

Chonk sneezes. And the phone rings, just long enough for Chonk to race for freedom, and for both my sisters to wake up.

It's ringing for me.

A bit of a surprise ringer too . . .

Baloo.

He asks how old am I, again?

I tell him (again).

He says thank goodness! What am I doing on Saturday morning? Only it's the last game of the season, against Our Lady of the Sorrows? He's just lost two defenders who've jiggered their wrists on the assault course at the Dads-and-Lads camp. So could I do him a good turn and turn out on Saturday?

I say I'm not in the cubs, so I can't do good turns.

He says I can be a provisional.

I say I'll be too old in two months.

He says no one will know.

I say I would know and anyway I haven't got a shirt because I had to hand back the one I used to wear because of Jamie Learmouth.

Baloo says he'll *give* me a shirt if I'll just turn up and turn out on Saturday morning.

I say I am getting my dog on Saturday morning.

He says Our Lady of the Sorrows beat us 17 nil last time, and that was with a full team and two subs.

I say I know that, but one of their players had a moustache last time, and Baloo should have used his best players.

He says he realizes that now.

I say the cubs weren't very friendly the last time I played, specially Jamie Learmouth.

He says they'll be very friendly on Saturday morning or he'll strangle them with their own neckerchiefs. I'm the best player he can think of in the whole town, so . . . please?

I say . . . All right.[1]

And I read stories to my sisters about happy
families and and girls called Deborah with teddies,
and the one about the disturbed boy who falls out
of bed into the kitchen, and one I make up as I go
along about a kid footballer who gets a call from
United begging him to turn out for the side in the
real Cup Final and when he does he . . .

I'm asleep, and Eliza and Madge are still awake,
when my dad comes in, singing, all garlic and
coffee and lemon at quarter to twelve.

We all sing.

I tell him I've been picked for Saturday morning.

He says good, but what about my dog? I say it
will be my last game ever for the cubs. Can't my
dog wait till the afternoon?

He says if it's as important as that he'll have to
come and watch the game himself.

Saturday morning is cool.[2]

Uncle Frank's last words are, 'Good luck on the
green and break a leg, and sock it to 'em, Julian!'

We leave him in charge of the packed Saturday
morning shop and set out in the green van. It's got
seats and belts now, and a sticker, SUPPORT

[1] *I want . . . gets!*
[2] *Real cool. The happy ending.*

YOUR PUBLIC LIBRARY.

I sit next to Dad and get some last-minute advice.

'Remember the main thing in sport,' he says, squodging third gear, 'is not the playing of the game. It's the *winning*.'

'What do you know about sport?'

He grins. 'I can swim a length? I've got me tracksuit?'

I can't grin back because I'm all adrenalin like a whippet.

I can feel it's going to be one of the great days.

There are huge crowds in the rec. There are over thirteen genuine cub spectators for a start, including Akela himself with a pot leg, and some dads already placing bets with Fireperson Rickaby.

Debbie Henderson is there too, and Natalie Thingy, Jenny Holmes, Eric Rickaby on his own, Norm and Mary Wilson poking carrots at people, some Squireses biting Maggie Hughes, Sandra Perry showing her knickers,[3] and Ali O'Shea and the daft kids showing off behind the bottom goal as the tension mounts.

Seven Our Lady supporters cower under a beach umbrella watching their seven lads, in clean new white tapping clean new footballs at each other. They look smaller than last time, except for the kid

[3] *Only nobody's looking.*

with the moustache.

I saunter to the changing shed, and do them a cub salute with the wrong sloppy arm.

Baloo is barking at them, 'Doing your best is what cubbing is about! If you don't do yours I'll be jiggered if I don't strangle you with your own neckties. Ah Julian, come in – '

He smiles as he says it's not only cubs who can be relied upon to help. In fact, he says, some young men who are not initiated set a better example of service than some who are.

He gives me my shirt.

The cubs clap paws.

Jamie Learmouth stands up to wish me a good game[4] and then leads the team out. I jog onto the pitch the other way to stretch, bend and prepare myself properly.

Even now there are still only seven Our Lady's. We could be in with a chance, this time.

Jamie Learmouth calls, 'I want you to stay back well in defence, Jazzer, and stop them getting an early goal like last time.'

'I'm going to roam.'

'I'm the capt– '

[4] *He's captain, of course, but only cos his birthday's late, and all the proper players have gone up into the Scouts or been jiggered some other way.*

I said, 'Football's all about being ready to go with it.'

'Yeah but –'

He looks skinny, as he stumbles to the centre for the toss. He lacks all credibility as a captain. Natalie Thingy must be thinking what a mistake she made when she swapped.

As Jamie Learmouth kicks off I notice the ref.

'Didn't know you were a um cub Julian?'

'Didn't know you were a um ref Mr Hills?'

'The real one broke his ankle at the Lads and Dads camp. But,' he whistles again, 'I know enough of the rules to know you have to get the ball over the centre line for the kick off um Jamie. So –'

I say, 'I'd better take it properly.'

'Don't let him ref!' Jamie whimpers.

Too late. I kick off, and roam.

It's a scrappy game, all throw-ins and kick and rush. Nobody knows how to make the ball do it, or how to get stuck in, and nobody's hungry.

I roam up front mainly, but I don't get any opportunities . . . apart from my two goals.[5]

Half Time
Us 2   Our Lady of the Sorrows 7
(Chandler 23 and 29)

[5] *!!!!!!!!*

I saunter the long way back to the shed to find Baloo already rollocking the whimpering cubs, sucking icy orange segments.

I chew gum like real footballers.

Baloo ends, '. . . rangle you with your own neckerchiefs. But *your* two goals were great Julian, specially the last one.'

I nod, and say quietly how goals are what football's about really. And it's not my business of course, I'm not Captain, James is, but I don't think we're hungry enough, are we? We need to get stuck in? Use the whole pitch? Let the ball do the work?

Baloo thanks me, and tells Jamie Learmouth to take note.

The wolves whimper out into the mud for the second half.

As I jog past them I notice Miss Day with Dad and the girls. I suddenly think how brave my sisters are. Braver than me. I haven't helped them enough. I love them.

But footballers don't wave at sisters in the middle of cup finals just because they're brave. I jog close, and then on, past a very pretty older girl who knows me.

'Here, Julian! Give us a kiss for luck?' She has shiny black hair like a spaniel's, and bright black eyes.

I jog past.

She shouts, 'I could fancy Julian as my toy boy.
Our Debbie's that lucky, look at his lovely legs.
I'm –'

I jog towards the centre.

'– Gloria from the naughty school!'

Mr Hills blows up and I re-enter the game, not
blushing at all.

Jamie Learmouth misses a penalty nine minutes
into the second half, after a little wolf cub whose
name nobody knows is carried bleeding off the
pitch crying for his mother.

The crowds shuffle, the rain thickens, and Mr
Hills blows up for full time after only quarter of an
hour. Nobody argues.

Final Score
Us 3   Our Lady of the Sorrows 12
(Chandler 23, 29, 35)

I call for three cheers for Our Lady, to show what
sport's all about.

Baloo gives me a right-handed shake, as if I'm a
proper cub, and says, 'The best result we've had
this season.'

'I did my best Baloo, and no cub could do more.'
I collect my clothes and I stride off for ever, just as
he's asking for the first volunteer to be strangled?[6]

[6] *Jamie Learmouth.*

Out in the rain, Gloria's already kissing the Our Lady with the moustache, but she winks over his shoulder at me as I go past and whispers, 'What you doing tonight big boy?'

'Walking the dog!' I reply, not blushing.

I ignore Natalie Thingy, already yelling about Jamie Learmouth missing his penalty and showing her up in front of everybody.

I let Debbie link arms with me, all the way back to my waiting family.

I sit in the front of the van next to my proud father. Miss Day, Eliza, Madge and Debbie crunch up at the back, saying how good I was.

Dad says, 'It's the best match I've ever been to Julian.'

Miss Day says, 'Your third goal was classic. Just like United's goal when we thrashed Wednesday in the cup, the same imaginative roaming use of the whole field, and then wallop . . . And a hatrick as well.'

'Thanks. But they're only little kids really aren't they?'

Debbie says, 'You're the one who's always wanted to play for them.'

'I want doesn't get.'

'You're getting what *you* want. You've played for the cubs, you're getting your dog and –'

Dad emergency stops. An ice cream van with

BEWARE CHILDREN is reversing at a crowd of children, to stop them going home till they've bought their Saturday gunge.

'I'm hungry,' Eliza says.

'And so are we,' says Miss Day.

Dad takes our messy orders for hamburgers, tomato sauce, hot dogs, taco sauce, gunge, white bread rolls etc.

And he brings back exactly what we've asked for, so we all get what we want.[7]

Miss Day leads the football chants through mouths gunged up with dead pig and sugar all the way home to German Street.

There is a woman standing outside The Magic Shop. She has two suitcases.

I don't realize at first.

Her hair is shorter, and black. She's fatter. She has a tiny baby strapped to her front.

'Look Dad!' I whisper, through hot dog and tomato sauce.

'I've looked.'

'Drive properly. Please? Don't muck it up now.'

I don't need to tell him. He looks in his mirror, slows to 15, signals, changes down to second, squeezes the brake, checks his side mirror, and slides perfectly in front of the shop into a space

[7] *Again!*

that should have been too small, but isn't, not today, please, please. Thank you.

He switches off the engine, pulls on the handbrake, puts the gears in reverse, switches off his indicator. And breathes very deeply.

'Amazing, Dad,' I say.

'I'm going to have to be a bit amazing now, aren't I?'

'You already *are*, actually!' I put my muddy hand on top of his, on the wheel.

He puts his other hand over mine. 'You're pretty amazing yourself.' Then he says, loud, 'You'd better all wait here. I think I've got a customer.'

He strokes his beard, unstraps himself without getting tangled, opens his door without trapping his fingers, walks in tracksuit and beard in front of his van without getting run over.

'My AMAZING FATHER!' I say.

No wonder she doesn't recognize him.

The football chanting stops.

Debbie breathes into my ear. 'What's happening?'

'My mother is.'

Debbie leans further into me. 'Her? She's come back? After all?'

I turn to Miss Day. She looks like the Miss Day we used to know before we knew her.

'Give Miss Day a cuddle, Eliza.'

Eliza says, 'Say please.'

Miss Day and I say 'Please,' together.

Madge says, 'Dwop ice cweam!' She's not supposed to be able to talk.

Debbie whispers, 'And have you noticed your mum's got the baby brother you've always wanted too? He looks about three months old, like the one next door to us that squeals.'

'How do you know he's a he?'

'Cos he's squealing and boys always squeal.'

I climb out. I notice Uncle Frank at the shop door looking puzzled, as if at last there's a trick even he'd not expected.

My mother joggles the baby. My father is telling her something.

I stare.

I'm chewing sausage gunge and white bread, and wearing a muddy cub football shirt. I live in a dirty flat with no garden.

And I'm getting my dog this afternoon.

There is not much here that my mother will . . . want.

She doesn't recognize me.

When she does, she holds out her arms.

I do not blush. My father is not blushing either.

My brother squeals.

I look back to the van. There are four faces at the window.

I don't know what *any* of us want, now . . . And we need to know, in case we get it.